CW00551028

First published 2022

Thinksheet Publishing

www.chrisjoneswrites.co.uk

Books by Christopher P Jones

NOVELS

Berlin Tales Trilogy:
Berlin Vertigo
Vanished in Berlin
Berlin Vengeance

ART HISTORY

How to Read Paintings
Great Paintings Explained

Christopher P Jones writes historical mystery fiction.

The first two instalments of the Berlin Tales include:
Part I. *Berlin Vertigo*
Part II. *Vanished in Berlin*

He is also a popular art critic and art history writer.

See more at www.chrisjoneswrites.co.uk

Thanks to Hema,
whose support has been unparalleled

BERLIN VENGEANCE

By
Christopher P Jones

Berlin Vengeance

PROLOGUE

Berlin Vengeance

1

At the break of dawn a freezing chill hung over the industrial wastelands of Berlin. Dozens of black crows pecked their way over acres of grassland. In the misty light, these barren fields could be mistaken for meadows of wheat, the way the low winter sun gave everything a golden glisten.

A man walked with his dog along a time-worn track. The ground beneath their feet had formed into one solid mass of mud and iced turf covered in a dusting of snow. Every so often the man broke into a whistled tune, sending pulses of white fog into the cold air.

The track carved through the open wilds that bordered the factory estates of the south-west limits of the city. Some buildings were either half-built or half-collapsed. Clusters of trees, once part of a great forest that covered the land, stood in isolated clutches, their ancestors long since cut down for wood and farmland to feed the metropolis of Berlin.

In the distance, it was possible to make out the Berlin-Drewitz plant of Orenstein and Koppel, manufacturer of steam locomotives. Beyond that was the nearby city of Potsdam and the wider Brandenburg landscape.

Further along the track, something jarred the

landscape. Nestled behind the trees was a large black object, marking the winter mist like a purple bruise on someone's skin. As the man went to take a look, he noticed the air was clogged with an acrid smell, something unnatural and different to the usual countryside scents of smoked wood and marshy dampness. It was the smell of smouldering rubber and metal.

He stopped. He called his dog to him and tethered the animal back on its leash. He went with caution as he drew closer. It was becoming clear that the thing up ahead was a burnt-out motorcar. He could see the chassis had collapsed and the car's four rubber tyres were sunk into the ground like a person buckled at the knees. The rear of the car had crumbled into a black dune, whilst the middle section was a smoking wreck of disintegrating charcoal.

The man saw that the earth around had been toasted bronze from the heat and the grass on either side of the road was torched down to stubble. The roof of the car had been bent and scorched by the flames. Pockets of smashed glass punctuated the windows whilst the flaps over the engine had opened up like the wings of an electrified bird.

As he peered through the smoked up glass, he was horrified to find what appeared to be the shape of a body inside. He saw the curve of the head first. Then he saw two wizened shoulders shrunk to a black pillar by the fire. The body was in the front seat facing forward, almost as if it could drive off in some ghoulish other-reality.

He moved around to the side of the vehicle where he could see more clearly. The body had been utterly ravaged by the heat. Little remained of the figure's legs but two charcoal stubs, like the piles of ash at the end of two cigarettes. The head was most shocking: a shrunken ball of bone the colour of ebony, where the skin had shrivelled back against the contours of the skull in melted folds. Any sign of life had been entirely gorged out from it, leaving nothing but a crumbling husk of black and grey. The smell that hung in the air now turned to burning rubber mingled with the tone of charred meat.

The dog then began to bark uncontrollably, for the animal knew there was something wrong. Its barks echoed into the open fields towards the row of factories in the far distance. On this lonely stretch of land, this flaking ember mass was stranded like a beached whale on the wild coasts of the Baltic Sea. And whoever was inside it, their final moments had been silenced by the deadly rage of a most hellish inferno.

PART I

2

Berlin. 30 January 1933

It had been a fierce winter. Snowdrifts had solidified into piles of crystallised ice on the roadside and it felt like the buildings had frozen solid. The cold evenings of Berlin were eased only by the temporary comforts of flashing neon lights and the lure of heated cinema auditoriums.

The city was ready for some good news: what had been a dismal few years were perhaps finally over. Tonight, those who could afford it ate meat and judged it appropriate to open a bottle of wine. They sat around their dining tables and dared to make plans for the year ahead. The job listing pages in newspapers seemed fractionally more prosperous than the day before, and the shops were busier too, as if there was suddenly more money in everyone's pockets. The *kneipes* and restaurants of the city bustled with customers, with some establishments reporting their liveliest trade since the turn of the decade.

Yet whilst a select few of society still lived in comfort, there were too many people out of work and facing starvation. Without enough money to feed their children, parents had begun to breed rabbits inside their houses to see them through the winter. And these weren't the only family pets that might later appear as the household dinner: cats and dogs had recently begun to vanish from the streets of Berlin at an alarming rate.

Something had to give. Change was long overdue and now the political landscape had shifted in the direction of Adolf Hitler, the new chancellor, a celebration was brewing. As the afternoon sun finally dipped behind the city rooftops, men in woollen frock coats and women in their best marten furs walked arm in arm towards the centre. Crowds began to gather. Excitement was trembling in the chilled evening air.

Erich Ostwald was one face among the many thousands. He made his way from Anhalter Bahnhof across Potsdammerplatz, walking and looking around in all directions. He took note of the blood-red banners emblazoned with swastikas that hung from the buildings, up to four storeys high. There were lines of rope tied between tree trunks to hold back the crowds as they watched the procession. And as it came – all five hours of it – the eager slap of the men's black boots never waned as they marched six-wide, each man proudly holding a flaming torch in his hand. The light from these flames outlined the city in complete clarity against the dark of night, even outdoing the neons and jazz bar spotlights in their blazing glow.

But more than anything else, Erich Ostwald was aware of the Nazi squadron leaders and their sentry men positioned to keep watch over the occasion. A posse of SA Brownshirts had already begun stopping people and verifying identities. Erich assumed that they were keeping an eye out for any Communist troublemakers who might throw a spanner – or something more explosive – into the works. And whilst he was no Communist, he had no plans to take any chances either. If he was stopped and asked his name he would have to lie about it, just as he had learned to lie about nearly everything in his life.

When he saw a huddle of Brownshirts stationed up ahead, he strode in the opposite direction, pushed a Juno cigarette into his mouth and crossed Königgrätzer Strasse towards the Brandenburg Gate.

He was a tall man. He gripped his cigarette firmly between his lips. A gush of dark auburn hair rose and fell in coils from his forehead. The cold air added a flush of red to his cheeks and gave the impression of impatience or mild agitation. He felt neither. His mind was clear and resolved. His only concern was for the task at hand, which he intended to carry out with the dispassionate air of a butcher over a fattened-up calf.

Half a mile further along Friedrich Strasse, Wolfgang Mayer climbed onto the uppermost rung of a wooden ladder. He had a hammer in his hand and was fixing one end of a red Nazi flag back into place after its moorings had drifted loose.

Mayer had come to Berlin to help with the celebrations. In fact he had travelled fifty miles – a day's journey on several buses – to be in the capital for the night. He considered it a privilege to lend his services in whatever way he could.

'Today is a great day,' he declared to at least three other passengers on the bus into the city.

Mayer was not a wealthy man but he held the principle that if the occasion demanded it he would be willing to spend a little money. He'd left his single-room house with its dusty oil lamps and damp-stained walls, and laid out a day's wages on the fare to Berlin. He'd budgeted a further week's wages for two nights at the Excelsior Hotel, one of the most expensive in the city. This was a special occasion after all. In his opinion,

9

Hitler was the sharp tonic the country desperately needed to heal itself. He was proud to call himself a German tonight.

He brought with him a bag of tools and had been assigned to look after the flags and banners of central Berlin. In exchange for his help, he'd been given a special gift: a ceremonial dagger with the words '*Alles für Deutschland!*' (All for Germany!) etched into the blade. He was delighted with his award, with its ivory grip and nickel silver crossguard. It was something he would treasure forever, and had already planned where he was going to hang it in his modest home.

Not being well off, in the summer of the previous year, when his work as a welder had all but dried up, he too had begun to breed rabbits. It had become popular all over Germany; a pleasant pastime too, that is until it came to the slaughtering part. Some people did it by breaking the rabbit's neck. Others achieved it by severing the animal's jugular artery. One of his neighbours in Neuruppin, where Mayer had spent the last five years of his life, opted for a bullet to the brain. Nobody could quite agree on which was the more civilised method. A quick death for the rabbit meant rather less guilt on the part of the owner. Anyway, after two or three of these kills, the guilt soon passed altogether. By October, Mayer had fifteen rabbits stored in iceboxes that he'd built himself from tin-lined crates and stacked up along the side of his house. There should be no way he would go hungry this winter.

Meanwhile, Erich Ostwald walked under the lit advertisements of the Kempinski Haus and glanced left and right. He was searching through the faces of everyone who passed, combing their features, looking for someone in particular. Every face that went by was

10

doused in shades of green and yellow by the flashing neons above. Each time he saw a face pass by, he wondered to himself if they had the particular face he was hunting for. His instinct would alert him once the moment came.

There were some basics that ruled out most people. They would have to be a man, of course. He would also have to be someone of roughly the same age and build as himself. An even match: that was the way it had to be. A more abstract consideration was the question of justification: he would prefer it if he could find someone who could be said to deserve it. That was one of the reasons he'd come into the city, because he was more likely to find someone of a more fitting character, especially tonight.

As the features of another Berliner came towards him, he took a moment to examine them from head to toe. Could it be you? But no, the similarity wasn't enough, the pieces didn't fit this time, and so he moved on and the moment evaporated like the gush of winter breath from the nostrils of a braying horse.

The January night was darkening and the streetlamps gave off a burgeoning glow as their filaments warmed. As he stalked the streets, his mood shifted between tension and resolution. He thought about dropping into the Café Vaterland and searching among its bubbling crowds. Surely he would find the right man there. Perhaps one of those unruly soldiers trying to get their hands on a prostitute. No. He had a more specific target in mind.

Then the Nazi procession began. Along the icy streets, columns of men dressed in uniforms paced and sang loudly. Members of the crowd raised their arms in allegiance. Some people called out the slogan, *'Deutschland, erwache! Jude, verracke!'* (Wake up, Germany!

11

Jew, drop dead!). Singing filled every street, along with the purr of military snares and the coarse honk of brass instruments. The air was so icy that the flaming torches popped and crackled, and the sparks that leapt up from the extreme clash of heat and cold danced in the air like tiny spirits. From a distance, the column of flames appeared like a glittering snake slowly prowling through the city. The buildings on either side vibrated under the glare of the orange light, as ten thousand men in customary brown shirts marched shoulder to shoulder for the celebratory hours.

A new era had begun. Hitler was chancellor of Germany. Only a successful general election stood in the way of a unified Nazi government. In far-off quarters, gunfire sounded excitedly.

Then, all at once, just as Erich returned along Königgrätzer, he saw a man perched at the top of a ladder. He watched him at work. He was roughly the same build and shape as him. And as Erich caught sight of his face, his curiosity grew more intense.

The ladder was leaning against a wall and the man on top of it was holding the corner of a flag emblazoned with the Nazi cross. The great red banner ran down the entire height of a building; the man on the ladder was tacking the corner of the banner to a wooden baton and then bracing it against the brickwork. He used a hammer to tack nails through the wood. There was something about him being up this ladder that gave him a stranded quality, as if he was lost in the strata above the street, alone and vulnerable. He was just right.

Erich placed himself at the foot of the ladder and called up in a friendly voice. 'Working hard?'

'Ya. Doing my bit.'

Erich noticed a tool bag on the ground. Inside was a wrench, a hand saw, some pliers, a pair of gloves and about five different sized screwdrivers. He saw something else too: a key to a room at the Excelsior Hotel. He couldn't believe his luck.

Erich called up again. 'Strong colour, this red,' he said.

'It certainly catches the eye.'

The man looked down at Erich who nodded back with a smile. The hunt was over. He'd now found his candidate.

3

Wolfgang Mayer climbed down the ladder and introduced himself. The two men chatted for a few minutes on the street corner then went to a tavern on Chausseestrasse. As they entered, Erich offered to buy the man a drink. 'It's the least I can do for all your dedication,' he said.

'I'm only doing what a million other Germans might,' the man replied.

Erich put his hand on his new friend's shoulder and led him inside. He swapped nods with the doorman, then took a table. He was glad of the recognition; it was important he was seen.

The Sing-Sing bar was one of the more bizarre establishments of the city: a restaurant modelled on a prison block, complete with jail-house bars and waiters dressed up as convicts. Erich had been there often. It had an uncertain atmosphere: on the walls, they had cut-outs of inmates trying to escape, with cartoon prison guards chasing them. There was even an electric chair based on 'Old Sparky' from the prison in New York. Clientele could sit and pretend to be buzzed to death while they waited for their drinks to arrive.

'You know, I never got your name,' Mayer said.

'Erich. Erich Ostwald.'

Saying his own name like that, just announcing it

plainly, felt strangely liberating. It was, he realised, the very last time he would refer to himself by it. He found himself repeating it, just to hear the two terribly familiar words leave his lips one more time. 'Erich Ostwald,' he said pensively.

He ordered them a beer each along with a plate of pork hocks to share. A red-headed cigarette girl came around; Erich bought a box and passed a cigarette to Mayer. The cigarette girl lent over and lit them both up with a single match.

He was privately pleased with his choice. Mayer was certainly the right height and the right size. These details were unconfirmed when he saw him up the ladder, but now they were together, shoulder to shoulder, his physical profile proved just right.

'I don't recognise you from these parts,' Erich said. 'I know a lot of people around here, but not your face.'

'I'm from Neuruppin,' Mayer replied. 'North of Berlin. It's a small place, and doesn't get many visitors.'

'And you've come to Berlin especially for the parade?'

'That's right. I volunteer for the Party. They asked me what my skills were and I told them that I'm useful with my hands, you see.' Mayer held up his palms as if to prove it. 'They want the demonstration to look solid and instructed me to go around and fix anything that I see. Flags and banners, whatever catches my eye.'

'Are you married?' – Erich rephrased his question – 'What I mean to say is, is your wife with you?'

'No, actually my wife died six years ago.'

That was lucky, Erich thought. A widower, someone with fewer loose ends, which would mean fewer people asking the wrong sort of questions.

'What about children?'

'We never got round to it, I'm sorry to say. What

about you?'

Erich's first instinct was to deny everything. But then again, what harm could it do, to spin a few tales, to play the game a little? It might help smooth the ride. If he could bring Mayer round to his side, it would make the rest of the evening go more simply.

'I never had any children with my wife,' Erich began, then moving the conversation on, he said, 'but just recently I started an affair with a very glamorous woman.'

'You did?' Mayer's eyes widened. He seemed to like the story.

'She's incredibly rich,' Erich went on. It felt good to say something brash and earthy like that. It was a complete lie, but what did it matter?

'You sly devil.' Mayer rolled his eyes and Erich tried to work out if his expression was one of admiration or envy. Maybe it was a mixture of both.

'Actually, I wouldn't recommend it,' Erich went on. 'I think she may be obsessed with me.'

They shared a chuckle between them, and with it, Erich began to feel a visceral excitement, as if he'd just picked out a chicken at a market and was about to watch it have its throat slit. A jolt of terrific fright ran through him, and he patted Mayer on the arm to calm himself down.

'Where did you meet her?'

Erich had no problem elaborating his tale. 'I travel a lot for work, you see. I'm a salesman by profession. Up and down the country I am. I like it but the evenings can get lonely. Then I met this lady in a bar one evening. She was luxuriously dressed and very fine-looking. I was an easy target because I am a bit insatiable, if you know what I mean. My appetite never seems to get fully satisfied. I sometimes think that's my biggest problem.

And there she was one night, this handsome woman with lust in her eyes. She was wearing this black chiffon dress, I remember, and she had long legs too. I like legs. I like them when they are slender, with just a little bit of muscle around the calves. Can you picture her? My slim seductress?'

Mayer nodded with glee. 'So you walked straight into her web?'

'I suppose I did. I couldn't help myself. Women seem to like me. With a face like this, how could she resist?' Erich smiled, clicking his glass with Mayer's.

'I wish I had that knack,' Mayer said. He rubbed his chin with the palm of his hand. Erich offered him another cigarette and Mayer took it with a relaxed air.

'Women have always bewildered me,' Mayer went on as he lit up. 'My wife was the only woman I ever met who I really connected to. I don't know why, but we just fitted together perfectly. It was the only time in my life that it happened like that.'

'I suppose you miss your wife?'

'Madly.'

The two men fell silent for a moment. As they took sips of their beer, Erich began to think of his old fiancée Ingrid and their child together. The boy would be four years old now – and still the two of them had never met. That would change soon, he hoped. Then he shook away the thought.

'Can you believe it's been that long?' Erich started up abruptly.

'What?' Mayer replied.

'Since the war ended.'

Mayer took on a more animated look. He seemed to like the change in topic. He brushed his hand over the bristles of his cropped hair and gave a snarling sort of grin. 'It's fifteen years ago now. Did you serve?'

Erich lied. 'Of course. You?'

'Eighth Army on the Eastern Front. Some of the best years of my life.'

'Passchendaele,' Erich responded in turn.

'You were at Passchendaele?' Mayer's eyes rolled again.

'Nineteen-seventeen. Not the best year of my life, I can assure you.'

'And afterwards! What a mess! You could buy guns and ammunition everywhere. Weapons and soldiers with no war left to fight. That shows you, doesn't it?'

'Shows you what?' Erich asked.

'We weren't finished, were we? I knew dozens of men who would have carried on the fight. Dozens and dozens.'

Erich nodded in agreement.

'Then what have we had since? Riots and strikes. Noise and complaining. Damned Communists. If I ever see another red ribbon, I swear I'll shoot the man wearing it.'

'Tomorrow we have a new start,' Erich said, fishing for the right words to keep Mayer on side.

'Quite right.' Mayer paused on a thought. 'Ever thought about revenge?' he said eventually.

'Revenge?'

'Retaliation. Settle the score.'

'Vengeance?'

'That's right.'

'Who with?'

'Anyone. Anyone who deserves it. I know an old Jew down my street who could probably do with some correction. He spends his whole day whining. He's not German. None of them are.'

'Is there any need for revenge after tonight? We've won, haven't we?'

18

'You mean Hitler? We'll see. Hindenburg still has too much power for my liking. No, what I'm talking about is more simple. I once saw a friend of mine lynched by a hoard of reds. Kicked black and blue he was. That's what the Jews want, of course, to let the reds in and depose of democracy.'

'And you'd like to give some pay-back?'

'I want to see someone get their just deserts. Nobody ever paid.'

'One last night to set the record straight?' Erich suggested. It wasn't what he planned, but he knew that with this style of talk he'd won his companion over.

'Exactly. Two old soldiers like us, what have we got to be afraid of?'

The stranger bent down to his bag of tools and rummaged around.

'This will help,' he said. He brought out a knife. He checked over his shoulder to be sure the burly doorman wasn't watching.

'I'd be careful with that in here if I were you,' Erich said.

Mayer slid the knife from its sheath and covertly presented the blade to Erich. It was new and glistening.

'Look at the eagle crest on the handle,' Mayer said, pointing.

Erich turned the object over in his hands. 'Very elegant.'

Mayer's eyes began to glow. 'Beautiful, isn't it? We could use it tonight,' he said.

'Tonight?'

'When we leave here. A quick bayonet between the ribs for some deserving soul.'

'That's what you have in mind, is it?'

'I was given this blade by the Party. It was a gift. It would be a shame not to baptise it.'

Erich handed the knife back. 'Whoever is in line for that is going to have a mighty shock.'

The stranger grinned. 'That's right.'

'Are you ready to do this?'

'After I've had enough of these I am.' Mayer held up his glass of cloudy beer and took another broad swig.

'We'd better order another one then,' Erich said, swallowing down his opinion of Mayer's plans. He lifted his arm to summon a waiter. 'We have a busy night ahead of us.'

4

Erich hurried them through their drinks and stood up. 'Shall we?'

'Let's go,' Mayer replied, taking the handles of his bag of tools.

Erich glanced down. Then it occurred to him that the tool bag could be a hindrance. It would be no good leaving it in the car. No, he had to get rid of it beforehand.

'Let's go to my car,' Erich suggested. 'I'll drive us. I've got a bottle of whiskey in there too. That should keep us going.'

'All through the night,' Mayer sparkled.

'Through to tomorrow morning if you've got the energy.'

Then Mayer had a second thought. 'But it might be a waste of my hotel room if I stay out all night.'

'Where are you staying?' Erich asked innocently.

'At the Excelsior.'

'Is that so? That's a nice place. Never been there myself, mind you. Too expensive for me.'

'Special occasions deserve special arrangements.'

'Why don't we take your tool bag back there first?' Erich insisted. 'Lighten the load a little?'

'Well, if you don't mind?' Mayer said.

They left the bar together and emerged onto the

21

night-time street. The city glow was casting the gothic spires of several churches into silhouette, now pressed flat against an orange-purple sky.

They walked two blocks towards Erich's motorcar. The rattle of a passing tram came and went, and in the distance a police siren wailed. There were still drums beating and the sound of brass tubas droning.

'Here it is.' Erich pointed to the black Adler saloon parked on the roadside.

'Fancy,' Mayer said. And with it, he rolled his eyes. Erich began to think there was something condescending in the way he did that. He wasn't sure. He didn't like the fact that he couldn't pin the gesture down.

'You don't have a car yourself then?' Erich asked.

'Not on my money. Besides, I don't go anywhere, not since my wife died…'

'How old are you, if you don't mind me asking?'

'I'm thirty-eight.'

'That makes us the same age. What month is your birthday?'

'September.'

'Mine's in August. That's close. Really close. That's good.'

'Good? Why so?'

'Oh, only – I notice such connections,' Erich said. 'I always say, there is no such thing as coincidence.'

'Funny,' Mayer said. 'My wife used to say the same thing.'

Erich smiled as he opened the car door. 'Here, put those tools on the back seat,' he gestured.

The two men got in.

'Do you like to gamble?'

Mayer shrugged. 'Me? I've been known to.'

'I tell you what. Before we get ourselves onto the

street, let's spend some money. We can take your bag back to the hotel, then we can go onto a casino. What do you think?'

'A casino? Not for me. I don't have anything to lose. It's been a tough year... Only gamble what you can afford. My wife used to say that too.'

'Don't worry. It's on me. I've had a good run this week. I made more money than all of last month. I feel like I'm on a roll. Let me pay.'

'No, I couldn't do that. I don't even know you.'

'I insist.'

'Well, if you insist.' Mayer looked ahead through the windscreen and allowed a private smile to edge onto his lips. Erich had the sense that Mayer was more excited about going to the casino than he let on, so he decided to stoke Mayer's fire by making up some fanciful details about where they were going.

'It's a wonderful little den I found just on the south edge of town. I swear, the casinos in the centre are all fixed. They've too much to lose, you see, but this little place, right on the outskirts, it's a real gem. I've never lost there. Every time I've been, I've come out a winner.'

'Sounds perfect.'

'It's a bit of a drive to reach, but it's worth it. They give you free drinks all night. I'm telling you, it's the best place for us.'

Erich drove towards the Excelsior Hotel. He toyed with Mayer by asking directions, even though he knew the way perfectly well. The passenger seemed to relax more, perhaps because telling Erich where to drive meant he was in control. In between giving directions, he started to talk about himself.

'I used to work as a security guard at a department store like that,' he said as they passed Wertheim & Tietz. 'That was when we lived in Munich. Every day I was

23

expected to look out for criminals and catch them. Beat the living daylights out of them if necessary. But it never happened. I just stood there all day, my back aching like a vice on my spine. But nobody ever stole anything. I suppose I did my job, in that case.'

'Good for you,' Erich said.

'I wouldn't work in that store though, mark my words. It's owned by Jews. Did you know that?'

Erich shook his head.

'Oh yes, practically any clothing shop you walk into, it's Jewish.'

A few minutes later, Mayer told Erich to slow down as the hotel was up ahead. Erich pulled the car over and Mayer jumped out, hauling his bag with him. He ran under the looming face of Anhalter station and across the square to the Excelsior. The night was dark and damp, with newspapers fluttering on the ground and the smell of steam trains and fried potatoes on the air.

Ten minutes later, Mayer was back in the car. Erich noticed he had changed his shirt and had splashed himself with cologne.

'I decided to leave the knife in the room,' Mayer said as he got back in the car.

'You've left it?'

'I decided. It didn't seem right carrying it around, on my person, so to speak.'

'No, you should have brought it.' Erich felt disgruntled. He intended to make use of the knife. He thought it could be evidence in his favour. 'Why don't you go in and get it again. What about its baptism?'

'They might search me at the casino. No point in taking that risk.'

Erich began to drive on. 'Yes, that's true.'

It was silly. They weren't even going to a casino.

'Don't worry, I'm useful with my fists,' Mayer said,

settling back in. 'I still want to crack a few rib bones, if you're with me?'

'Oh yes.'

'So tell me about this rich woman you've started up with,' Mayer said, hardly hiding his excitement as they drove through the night.

Erich was pleased to return to the topic. It was the first time in years he'd been so open with another person – even if the details were completely fabricated.

'I wish I could make her see reason.'

'She's a bit overbearing then?'

'Absolutely. Her family know about it too and they all insist that I do the right thing and make an honest woman out of her. The trouble is, none of them know I'm already married, and I don't suppose they'd be too pleased if they found out.'

'Sounds a bit heavy,' Mayer said, grinning to himself.

'And that's not the end of it. I've got another woman in Leipzig. She's got a shocking temper and doesn't stand for me being away for more than a fortnight. I don't have any reason to go to Leipzig anymore, not after all my customers there dried up, but I'm back and forth to that city every other week. I'm spending money like there's no tomorrow. Hotel bills, petrol, dinners out in restaurants.'

'Why not just put an end to it?' Mayer said.

'I would, but I'm too much of a coward.'

'You've got to put a stop to that – cowardice I mean. Never let a woman do that to you.'

'Women. They're my weakness. My way of dealing with a difficult woman is to string her along until she gets bored of me. It usually works. It would be easier if I could just disappear. If only they all thought I was dead.'

With this last sentence, Erich felt himself sailing a little too close to the wind. Yet it excited him to expose himself like that. Besides, why shouldn't he tell the truth to Mayer? His life would be easier if he could disappear. They were practically friends now, and if he couldn't tell his friends what life was like for him, then who could he tell?

Mayer looked over. 'How far is the casino?' He began to rub his hands together to make a show of his expectation.

'Not much further.'

The city centre was behind them now. They drove through the long silence of the suburbs, a nocturnal setting punctuated by the occasional street lamp or late-night shop front. Erich began to think it was time to brace himself. The social hours were finished with. He was satisfied. He'd done well. He'd managed to get Mayer to trust him. Now it was time to turn his mind to the business at hand. It was too late to reappraise or to have second thoughts about what lay ahead. It was time to do what he had spent months planning.

He pulled the car over to the side of the road and slowed down to a crawl. The task now was to find the side-turning he had previously decided on. It had been daylight then and it was easy to determine. It was a different matter now, and in the excitement of the moment he was having trouble deciphering his whereabouts.

'I don't know this area,' Mayer said, sensing Erich's heightened state.

'I'm just looking for the turning,' Erich replied.

'It's been years since I went gambling,' Mayer said. 'My wife wasn't too keen on me losing money. But the thing is, you don't always lose, do you? That's what she didn't understand. Sometimes you win. That's what risk is all about.'

'If you can be quiet for a moment,' Erich said. He

was hunched forward over the steering wheel and his eyes were squinting.

'I was just saying, my wife...'

'I don't want to miss this turning.'

'Is there a road sign to look out for?'

'I said shut up.'

'Right. Sorry.'

'Don't make me tell you again.'

Mayer looked out of the side window. He began to think there was something wrong with the present circumstances. He wanted to know where they were, but from the corner of his eye he could see that Erich's demeanour had changed.

Erich now turned the car onto an anonymous side road that ran beside a tall wire fence and some old allotments. Erich knew the turning because there was a tram-stop opposite.

Ahead of them it was as dark as a dense forest. The only thing Mayer could see was the vague silhouette of a factory building slipping by in the distance. There were no lights, and after a few moments, the road turned from a smooth surface into a bumpy track.

Instead of the question he wanted to ask, Mayer found himself asking, 'What's wrong Erich?'

'Nothing.'

'Are we lost?'

'I'm taking a shortcut, that's all.'

Mayer crossed his arms over his chest. 'What's the name of this casino?'

'I forget.'

'You don't know the name of it?'

'No.'

Mayer fell quiet. He looked over and caught Erich's eye. 'We're not going to the casino, are we?' he said.

'No,' Erich said. And with that single word, he knew

27

that time was running out and his plan would have to happen very soon.

'Then where are we going?' Mayer looked to his left and took note of the door handle. If the car slowed down any more, he decided, he would grab the handle and throw himself out. He didn't know what was happening, but he had good instincts and knew when it was time to leave a situation.

Erich didn't respond. He'd found the turning but that wasn't the end of it. Now he had to get to the correct spot along the lane. He was looking for a telegraph post. Twenty yards beyond it there would be a dark green tarpaulin on the ground.

He glanced over at Mayer. He could tell he was getting edgy. He realised he needed to keep the car moving at a pace, and that didn't make the task of finding the telegraph pole any easier. It was pitch dark, even with the headlamps turned to their brightest setting, but just then, up ahead, he saw it. The telegraph pole and beyond it, the green tarpaulin hiding the can of petrol.

He pulled the car to a sudden stop. The tyres slipped on the icy mud and the vehicle juddered as it came to a rest. For a moment, both men looked at each other expectantly, wondering what the other was going to do next.

Erich turned off the engine. 'We're here,' he said.

5

Mayer didn't utter a word. Instead, he snatched at the chrome door handle in an attempt to escape. But it snapped back as Erich put his arm across his chest and braced him against the seat. With his other hand, Erich reached behind and tried to grab hold of the wooden mallet that he'd deliberately stashed on the floor beneath the passenger seat.

Of all the steps he'd previously conceived in his imagination, this one was the most important. The mallet was vital. His hand groped in the dark for the wooden hammer. As he did, he gripped Mayer across the larynx, forcing his head into the back of the seat. Mayer slid down. He gasped, trying to call out but struggled for air. Erich now turned, kneeling on the driver's seat, pressing the victim's throat even harder. Mayer grappled at Erich's neck as he tried to lift his weight off him.

The struggle was messier than Erich had anticipated. It took every ounce of his strength to keep Mayer pinned in his seat. Still, he felt he had the stronger position. To see Mayer struggle like this, to witness the fright in his eyes and to feel his body tense up, made it all the more natural for his own violence to wake up.

It was at this point that a knife appeared. The flash of silver caught Erich by surprise. Mayer still had the Nazi blade with him after all. He'd lied.

Mayer had managed to pull the knife from his pocket. He held it in one hand with a frantic grip, attempting to turn it in Erich's direction. Erich tried to knock it out of his palm but Mayer moved his hand too quickly. He took hold of the blade more firmly now and thrust it towards Erich's face.

Erich let go of Mayer's throat and deflected the incoming weapon. He pushed Mayer's hand so it clattered against the dashboard. The knife was still in his grip as Erich tugged his arm down. The blade turned and drove back towards Mayer and punctured his side just below the waist. Mayer cried out in pain and the knife fell to the darkness of the floor.

Finally, Erich found the mallet from behind him. He brought it forward and swung it in Mayer's direction. He was aiming at his head but Mayer shifted over so it landed as a thump on his shoulder.

It didn't seem like much of a blow, yet it was good enough to leave Mayer momentarily dazed. A second swing of the mallet caught him on the eyebrow. But if this one was supposed to incapacitate him, it had the opposite effect. Mayer's hands shot up and grabbed hold of the face of the mallet. He wrestled with it as he might tackle the jaws of an angry dog coming at him.

The restricted space of the car's interior now turned to Mayer's advantage. He pushed the mallet away, thrusting Erich backwards, wedging the driver up against the steering wheel. Erich felt the flesh around his ribs pinch against the wheel.

Fortunately for Erich, he decided to let go of the mallet, which once released, sped across the space of the car with Mayer's full weight behind it. It struck the driver's window and smashed straight through. Mayer lay stretched across the front seats, at which point Erich opened the door and slid himself out onto the muddy

30

track. Standing up, he wrenched the mallet out of Mayer's hands and in a short, stabbing motion, clubbed Mayer about the head. Mayer's entire body was rendered limp.

Erich had no inclination to deliver a second blow. He went straight to the green tarpaulin ten paces ahead which remained undisturbed. He grabbed the can of petrol beneath it, unscrewed the cap and began to douse the petrol over the car. The smell was so pungent and he thought that Mayer might be roused by it. Several glugs of the toxic liquid had sloshed onto Mayer's head, making his hair wet and oily. Mayer remained completely motionless.

Erich went quickly to the front of the car. First, he prised away the registration plate and threw it ahead of the car. Then he lifted the engine flaps. His fingers were slippery with petrol and it took him a moment to loosen the feeding pipe between the tank and the carburettor.

He retrieved the petrol can and was halfway through emptying it when it dawned on him that Mayer had to be moved. So he put down the can, and as he reached over the body, he noticed the Excelsior Hotel room key was hanging out of Mayer's pocket. That was useful, he thought, as he removed the key and dropped it into his own pocket. Luck was in his favour.

It was important to manoeuvre Mayer's frame into the right position, first by turning him over, then by lifting up him by the armpits. The legs were the worst part. He had to crunch them into the gap beneath the steering wheel. It reminded him of the time he chopped down an old tree in his parent's garden and had to dispose of it by cutting it up to make a bonfire.

Erich now began to think he should finish Mayer off before setting the car alight. It would mean an act of mercy so Mayer wouldn't feel the heat of the flames if he happened to wake up. Erich thought he could suffocate him without too much trouble. And yet, death by asphyxiation was not how it needed to look. What he needed was for Mayer to be sat upright in the driving seat for the effect to be convincing.

Then he looked up. Someone was coming.

At first there was a single hovering point of light in the far distance, then as it drew nearer, the light separated into two circular beams that traced their reach along the shrubs and fence posts that lined the track. It was a pair of car headlamps moving towards him.

Erich panicked. He had to act quickly and disappear. He threw the rest of the petrol onto the vehicle, lit a match and tossed it towards the car. With the potent fumes in the air and heat still in the engine, a flame rose instantly. He watched the blaze grow, before taking the green tarpaulin and thrusting it onto the fire. Then he dashed along the dark track with his own silhouette dancing ahead of him, lit by a halo of pulsing orange.

At fifty paces clear from the car, he suddenly realised he still had the wooden mallet in his coat pocket. It was too late now to return and throw it onto the fire as he always intended. The very purpose of choosing the mallet was in order to burn the evidence afterwards. He attempted to break the object in half with his bare hands. This proved useless, so he smashed the mallet against the trunk of a tree, pounding the head once, then twice. With the third blow the mallet broke into pieces. The handle shattered into several shards, which he discarded into a tangle of holly bushes. He picked up the decapitated head of the mallet and scouted around for a place to dispose of it. The answer presented itself in the form of a small marshy pond that emerged out of the darkness on his right, its waters as black and thick as ink.

He had no time to lose. He took hold of the wooden

block and slung it, long and hard into the water. He watched as it landed with a splash and then quickly sunk into the pond. He waited to see if the object would float back to the surface but it remained submerged.

A few moments later, a shaft of heat shot up behind him as the car exploded. The flash of white illuminated the land for a mile in every direction, as if the moon had just flickered like an electric bulb. He ran and plunged into a sidetrack that furrowed beneath a row of trees.

With the metal can in his grip, it clanged against the branches as he went deeper into the snarled undergrowth. He was conscious of his feet as they rampaged over the tangle of brambles that lay across the ground. He dropped the petrol can. The light from the burning car was diminishing now as he burrowed further into the wood, until at once he emerged into an open field whose stubble of corn was lit by a row of distant streetlamps.

Every muscle in his body was put towards crossing that field and finding his way back to town. From there, a late-night train north, a few months living invisibly on the coast, then a new life under a new name.

Erich Ostwald was no more.

PART II

6

It was late in the evening by the time Arno Hiller ventured out onto the streets of central Berlin to see what all the fuss was about. The frosty roads glistened like shellac and above the buildings a strange orange glow loomed, spreading an unearthly radiance into the black sky.

He found himself surrounded by the ferment of a city in the throes of a party. The torchlight procession that hailed the arrival of Chancellor Herr Hitler snaked through the pillars of the Brandenburg Gate and onto Wilhelmstrasse. The people called out and clapped as the parade passed by. The sound of ten thousand jackboots marching over the winter cobbles had the ring of an enormous orchestra banging a lone marching drum.

Children perched on their parents' shoulders and others clambered up lampposts to see beyond the sea of heads. *Germany Awake!* was the rallying cry. It was written on every banner and pasted onto every hoarding. Red flags with golden finials floated through the air. At the windows of first-floor apartments, faces were pressed to the glass, where all manner of people gathered in a single frame to catch a glimpse of this night-long spectacle.

Arno moved through the crowds. He didn't know how to feel about his city any more. The atmosphere had changed. It was as if the entire place was a warbling reflection in the glass window of the Wertheim & Tietz department store. It seemed unreal and foreboding, like a terrible dream.

He made it to the Chancellery and raised himself up on the steps of a nearby building. Over the heads of what seemed like a million people he saw the figure of Hitler himself, waving and saluting from the stone balcony. All the speeches, all the radio performances, all the electioneering, had culminated in this moment. The new chancellor stood erect and still like a statue. Others lined up next to him. Göring. Frick. Von Papen. They lurked in the background, soaking up the cheers that rang out.

Arno dipped his head beneath the ripple of another swastika flag. The news these people were rejoicing in, he didn't feel the same excitement for. He walked on with his shoulders hunched and his hands deep inside his coat pockets. To his mind, there was something gratuitous and frenetic about the celebrations, as if half the country had lost their minds. The optimism of the crowds suggested that life in the city would get better from now on, but he had other expectations.

He decided to go home and leave the city to their party. He took a tram back to Hallesches Tor and returned to his room above Café Kaiser. It was so cold tonight, his attic room seemed more chilled than ever. His windows had iced up on the inside and snow melted through the roof tiles onto the bare wooden floor. He'd moved his bed to the middle of the room to avoid being dripped on and angled it so it faced the stove, which he would leave burning all night through as he had done for the past month.

But he didn't mind because tonight was different. Tonight he had something of his own to celebrate, something that was nothing to do with the inauguration of Adolf Hitler. Tonight was his very last night in the attic room – he was moving out. And moving up. For once in his life he had a regular salary and he could finally afford an upgrade in his circumstances.

With his coat and hat still firmly on, he pulled out wurst and schinken, some pumpernickel and kümmelbrot, a thick block of cheese, an apple and a bottle of wine. He poured out a large cup for himself and raised a toast to the half empty attic room.

'Here's to the future!'

He lifted his cup and smiled to himself. Then, for the next twenty minutes, he gorged on the food and sank three cups of wine in succession.

'Tomorrow will be better.'

As he said the words, his mind was irresistibly drawn to the girl he once loved. Still loved. Monika. He wished she was with him now. It had been two years since they were last together. His heart ached like a bruise whenever he thought of her and how she was so far away from him – somewhere inside the glittering dream of New York.

He raised his cup to her and in a soft voice said, 'I'll never forget you,' before lifting his feet onto the bed, wrapping the covers around him and instantly falling asleep.

7

The following morning, Arno pulled out the old suitcase he'd borrowed from his sister and began to stuff it with clothes, books and the three beer bottles he hadn't yet consumed. Everything else – the bicycle with its flat tyre, the bedclothes, the washing line with socks still pegged to it – he'd leave for the next tenant to enjoy.

He said his goodbyes and carried the bulging case down the stairs. As he emerged onto the open plaza, he glanced up at the tall apartment blocks that surrounded the square, with its hotel and café signs that looked washed-out in the morning light. Yes, he was pleased to be leaving. This district had always felt like something of a mixed blessing. The rent was cheap, but with it came an unpredictable edge. It seemed like everyone he met was either on their way up or on their way down. Some folk dazzled with hope for their own futures. Others were pickled in depression and seemed beyond saving.

The suitcase was too large to carry on his motorbike – an old four-stroke v-twin engine he'd acquired from his brother-in-law – so he would have to travel by tram. He lit a cigarette and stood mindlessly watching a steady trickle of people pass over the canal bridge ahead of him. There were always people on the move in Berlin, especially with so many people being uprooted at the moment, no matter what time of day you happened to look.

A few minutes later, a column of men carrying Nazi flags came over the bridge too. They held a great banner over their heads that read 'Death to Marxism.' Arno paused to watch the motley parade, studying the men as they passed. With Hitler in the Chancellorship, what might once have been a mixture of anger and vague excitement on the men's faces had now solidified into something more robust. The celebrations from the day before had built a momentum of vitriol that was sure to inspire many more impromptu parades like this: little more than local enthusiasts who had joined together to fashion their own neighbourhood rally. As they marched along the road, they received a chorus of support from well-wishers, along with the occasional heckle of abuse from an invisible dissenter.

Just then, at the foot of his building, Arno ran into one of his neighbours, a corpulent woman from the floor below.

'Fancy joining the march!' she cackled, grinning wildly.

Arno raised his eyebrows as he trod on his cigarette.

'Leaving us are you?' she asked, glancing down at the suitcase. The woman had large square shoulders and a mountainous bosom. Despite the freezing cold, she was wearing nothing but a white undergarment and a pair of dirty-pink slippers.

'I can finally afford to move out, so I'm heading into the centre,' Arno responded as he swapped his suitcase between arms.

'Shame. A real shame.'

'Actually, I'm pleased to be going.'

'What about my daughter?'

'Your daughter?'

'Spare a thought for her. She is very fond of you.'

41

'Oh, I didn't realise.'

The woman's face flickered for an instant.

Arno pictured the daughter, remembering a girl with short black hair and a dress with purple flowers stitched through. She was pretty in a pallid sort of way. They'd spoken only once, when she'd told him she had a passion for Egypt and would do almost anything to have lived in the time of the pharaohs. Her dream was to climb a pyramid and look out across the miles of desert from the very top.

'If you ever come back, make sure you drop in on us,' the woman said. It was the warmest thing she'd ever said.

'Maybe I will. Please pass on my best to her,' he responded.

The woman let loose a grotesque smile, crooked and wide. 'She'll like that,' she said as a look of dishonour bloomed in her eyes. 'I'll tell her you will miss her,' she said laughing. 'She'll like that!'

Arno took up the weight of his luggage and moved on. Finally, a tram pulled up and he boarded to head north. His new address was close to Potsdamer Platz and even afforded a modest view over the Tiergarten park. With his new salary, he could afford an apartment that had hot and cold plumbing and electric lights in every room. The stove was twice the size of his last one and in much better condition. It would be like living in luxury by comparison.

When he arrived at his new quarters, he dropped his case onto the bed and wandered around the apartment. Today his larder was empty, so he went out to find a restaurant to eat some lunch. At a tiny place where customers stood to eat, he gorged on mettbrötchen with a large gherkin on the side.

After eating, he walked among the wintry forest of

the Tiergarten and looked up at the naked tree branches that were lit by a low winter sun. With their leaves long since shed, every twist and turn of every tree branch was visible, as the harsh light made the whole park seem like a stage of petrified stone.

He walked until the sun had gone and the evening chill tightened its grip. On returning to his apartment, he hooked his coat on the rack and went to his suitcase. He took out a photograph of Monika and positioned it on a little table so that he could it see from his bed. Then he dug out an envelope marked 'International Mail.' It was the last letter he'd received from her, nearly six months ago already:

Dearest Arno,

Summer has arrived in New York. They say it can get very hot here, so we are bracing ourselves.

I've found work for myself as a typist at the National Council of Jewish Women. It's exciting and the girls are nice and they seem to like me. Perhaps they think my accent is entertaining!

At the weekends I go roaming around with my camera. I think of you walking around Berlin and me in New York, as if we could be wandering around together.

My heart breaks because my memories of you are fading. I wish I had an image of you I could look at. Your face is losing its details, like when I twist my camera lens out of focus.

Sorry this letter is short. I'm writing on my lunch break. Actually, this may be my last letter for a while. Father has found out that I've been writing to you and has told me I must stop. Mother has permitted it until now, but father is old-fashioned and strict. You know him – he doesn't trust anyone where his precious daughter is concerned!

I'm sorry. We will always keep in contact somehow, won't we?

43

With love always and forever,
Monika

He put the letter back inside the envelope and remembered the day they said goodbye, the very last time he set eyes on her. They were standing at the end of her street. She was travelling to Hamburg the following day. Oddly, they were both overcome with sudden shyness. As she whispered, 'I have to go now,' he had no other instinct than to kiss her, slowly and deeply. At first, the ridges of her lips were cold from the wintry air. He felt the resistance of her mouth as he held his kiss in place. But gently she relented, allowing her muscles to soften and her lips to part slightly with his. Then she went back to her house and he never saw her again.

8

The next day, Arno left his new apartment for the police headquarters on Alexanderplatz. It was a palatial looking building, also known as the Red Castle on account of its tall red-brick walls and lancet-style windows. He had walked by it hundreds of times but hardly imagined that one day he would be working there.

He'd been called to a meeting with the lead detective of the Central Homicide Inspection unit, Karl Nummert. When Arno arrived, Nummert was sat on the other side of his great oak-wood desk that must have weighed half-a-tonne.

'It looks like we finally have a job for you,' the detective said as he pulled on a cigarette.

'Well, I am ready,' Arno replied curtly. It was frustrating having to spend the past few months observing other officers and shuffling papers in the wing of the Kriminalpolizei known colloquially as 'Purgatory.'

'A motorcar with a body inside,' Nummert went on, 'was found in an industrial zone in the south-west. Out in the sticks, halfway to Potsdam. A man and his dog came across it early this morning.'

'Near Potsdam, on the edge of Drewitz?'

'Yes.'

'I used to work around there,' Arno replied. 'I know it well.'

'At the locomotive plant wasn't it?'

'Orenstein and Koppel,' Arno confirmed.

'That's why we're sending you. It should help that you know the terrain.'

'Do we know who was inside the car?'

'No. The vehicle was burnt out. The body too. It's nothing but charcoal.'

'Are there any other details?'

'Not much. The local police have asked us to take a look. They're sending a couple of men down there today to have a scout around before the coroner comes to remove what's left of the body. There's no particular reason to think it's anything other than bad luck for the driver. But the way things are at the moment, every death has to be treated with circumspection.'

Arno stood up.

'And there was one other thing...' Nummert said.

'What?'

'Actually, I'll let you find out.'

'Interesting. Do I get any support?'

'See what you can find first.'

'And if it's a murder case?'

'Let me be honest with you. If you were anybody else we'd assign a team to investigate. You'd even get a dog handler.'

Arno thought of the muzzled Alsatians he'd seen straining on a leash with the other men. He'd like to have the status the animal conferred if nothing else.

'But I'm a different case,' Arno replied.

'You're the one that slipped through the net. By rights, you shouldn't have that badge of yours. That means we have to be cautious with you. No murder wagon I'm afraid.'

Arno forced a smirk as he gritted his teeth. The murder wagon was a specially designed unit kitted out with radio and photographic equipment that travelled out to crime scenes, most often when there was a dead body involved.

'So I'll be going out alone?'

'You've got to prove your credentials.'

Arno had little choice but to agree. He left the headquarters and went to find his motorbike. He rode through the chilled streets of Berlin with a leather helmet over his head and two flaps strapped beneath his chin. The icy air grazed his jaw like windburn and his fingers soon began to bite with cold. Across the city, the winter was still in full grip. Dagger-like icicles hung from doorways and fluffed-up pigeons sat hunched on the ledges appearing frozen to the spot. Lines of washing hung out to dry had solidified into stiff white boards.

It was a long way out of the centre, the sort of gutted wasteland that the frosty winter only made more savage. The track was dotted with iced-up puddles that whined and split under the weight of his motorbike as he rode over them. He pulled up his bike a distance before the burnt-out wreck and walked the remainder on foot. Already, two officers from the local Potsdam force were circling the black ruin and probing it with sticks they'd evidently picked up from the nearby trees.

Arno decided he would take charge of the scene. 'My name is Detective Arno Hiller,' he called as he approached. 'I'm the investigating officer assigned to this case from the Berlin Criminal Police.'

The two policemen stopped and looked up, swapping dumb glances and making no attempt to conceal their snide smiles.

'The first thing I want is an inventory of everything here,' Arno proceeded.

The two men made no move. They were both considerably older than Arno and it was clear that they

47

didn't take kindly to being told what to do by someone so young.

'Well? What are you waiting for?' Arno said as he got closer. 'Get to it.'

'We don't answer to you,' one of them said.

'We're waiting for the coroner to come,' said the other.

'This could be a murder scene. Nothing is to be touched. No evidence is to be removed until I give my word.'

'There's nothing here to say it's murder,' one of the policemen replied confidently.

'Let me be the judge of that.'

'Accidental if you ask me. Vehicles like this, they're prone to overheating and catching fire. Looks to me like they got stuck in the mud, the driver over-charged the engine, and that was the end of that.'

Arno glanced at the burnt-out car.

'Know a lot about motorcars, do you?' the officer asked sarcastically.

'Enough,' Arno replied. He passed the policemen and toured the car in a circle. In fact, he knew next-to-nothing about motorcars, but he'd long since learned that bluster can count just as much as knowledge, so long as you know how to deploy it.

The policemen's gaze followed Arno until he spoke again. 'When was the vehicle discovered?'

One of the policemen referred to his notebook and read, 'Reported to have been first seen after dawn yesterday.'

'It must have burned through the night, even with the current temperatures,' Arno thought to himself. Then he spoke out loud. 'Why would someone be driving along this track? Where would they be going?'

'Scenic drive?'

The two police officers looked at each other and began sniggering.

'Where does this road lead? Does it go to one of the factories?'

'There's an old farm about a mile away. Abandoned now. The farmer probably sold his land to make way for the foundry.'

One of the police officers, the one who was doing most of the talking, stepped forward, tapping the end of his stick against the frosted ground ahead of him.

'People take wrong turns all the time,' he said as he adopted a wiser tone. 'He was probably an old man who couldn't see more than ten yards ahead. The poor sod got lost. It was dark. He got stuck. Next thing his motor was up in flames.'

Arno looked at the flank of the car, which was little more than a heap of embers. Taking the stick off the policeman, he prodded it into the car door. It was like pushing a knife into a sponge cake.

He looked into the shell of the car. The wizened form of the body inside was gently hunched forward and contracted inward as if the heat of the blaze had curled everything in on itself. There was no discernable expression in the figure; the face was nothing but a screwed up ball of mangled bones, all of it blackened to a cinder with smoke and heat.

Arno swallowed. It was impossible to see any form of human character except in the broad stump at the steering wheel. He stepped forward and peered closely at the side of the figure. He felt an odd protectiveness towards it, with an unexpected drive to deliver justice for this poor wretched corpse.

He retreated as he paused in thought. Then he turned back to the policemen. 'What I don't understand is why they didn't get out of the car.'

'Excuse me, sir?'

'The driver. Why didn't they get out of the car? Surely, they'd have to be unconscious or trapped in to be engulfed by the flames?'

'It could have happened quickly. If petrol leaked from the engine, these things can take a matter of seconds.'

'Maybe the car exploded,' the other policeman added. 'That would explain it.'

Arno looked carefully around the vehicle. It was a messy, tangled heap of ash, merged with those parts of the car that had survived the fire: the curved wheel arches and the rear chassis. He searched the engine box at the front which was scalded. Several yards ahead, the car number plate lay more or less intact on the muddy track.

'The number plate was hardly touched by the fire,' Arno surmised.

'If there was an explosion, it could easily have been thrown clear.'

Arno found it hard to believe. He took out a notepad and wrote down the number on the plate. 'If the car was registered, we can trace the owner. Has it been reported stolen?'

The two officers shrugged their shoulders.

'Oh,' one of the officers woke up. 'The man with the dog, the one who found the car in the first place, he mentioned something about an empty petrol can somewhere in the woods over there.'

'Didn't you take a look?'

'We're supposed to wait for the coroner.'

'Fine. You wait here. I'll go.' Arno left the officers and began along the dirt lane towards the line of trees in the distance.

'We're just following orders,' one of the policemen

50

called after him.

Arno ignored the comment and walked on. When the track began to peter out, a narrower footpath led off through a thicket of hazel trees. As he followed the path, his shoes slipped on the melting mud underfoot, forcing him to grab a tree trunk to keep his balance. He searched around and after about ten minutes he found the petrol canister. It was white, about the size of a briefcase and full of dents. Its screw-lid was missing. When he lifted the spout to his nose, the smell of petrol was vivid and fresh.

He took the can back to the car wreck and held it up for the police officers to see. The policemen nodded, then turned away to light a cigarette each. Great gusts of wintry smoke rose up from their cupped hands as they lit up.

Arno examined the car again. He picked up a stick and used it to rake through the debris. He went round to the passenger side and probed his stick into the waste, keeping away from the body so as not to disturb it. Then he saw something in the grey embers. It glinted. It was a shard of silver among the ash. He nudged it and then brushed the ash away with the stick. The shard became a blade. He put on a pair of gloves, then used his stick to drag the object toward him and picked it up. It was a knife. The blade was around six inches long. The handle appeared to be made of ivory, which was tarnished by the fire, but the metal blade and crossbar were mostly intact.

He looked behind him. The local officers were facing the other way, so he took the chance and slipped the knife into his pocket.

'Any sign of the coroner?' he called out.

'Could be another hour yet,' one of them turned and replied.

'I want you to keep everyone else away.'

'Like who?'

'Anyone who turns up.'

'Like a journalist?'

'Exactly like a journalist.'

'Too late,' one of the officers said.

'Why do you say that?'

'There was one here twenty minutes ago. Whilst you were in the woods.'

'A journalist? From where?'

'He said he was from *Der Angriff.*'

Arno knew the publication well. It was a Nazi newspaper. Joseph Goebbels was the editor.

'What did you tell him?' Arno asked.

'What's there to tell? He sniffed around for a bit and made a few notes.'

Arno went round to the front of the car and prised the registration plate from the ground. Along with the petrol canister, he took the plate with him. 'If anyone else arrives asking questions,' he said to the two officers, 'turn them away. Nobody else is to come near or disturb the site. I'm leaving for now. I'm going to find out more about our cremated friend.'

9

Arno rode back to Alexanderplatz with the petrol canister and registration plate in his motorbike panniers. The knife he'd picked up was wrapped in his handkerchief and sat bobbing inside his coat pocket. He knew that if he was more established within the agency he would have all this ferrying around done for him. There would be an investigative team who would gather the evidence in the proper way, who would engage the pathologist unit and sift through the archives on his behalf. But all this, Arno would have to do himself.

Some said he wasn't experienced enough to be part of the Kriminalpolizei. They complained he hadn't been through the appropriate training and that it was unfair on others that he'd leap-frogged the twelve-month internship. The fact that he hadn't attended criminal college in Charlottenburg was reason enough for some to dismiss him as a rogue amateur, assisted into Kripo either by luck or untold nepotism.

And yet – the counter-argument ran – what he lacked in qualifications he more than made up for in experience. Nobody else his age had such a chequered history. No one else had ever run with the Ringvereine gangs of Berlin and had been paid in secret envelopes of cash to transport illegal goods across the city. Nobody else had been mixed up in the violent war between the

Communists and the fascists, or been recruited as an agent for the Prussian Police and lost the love of his life for his efforts. There was no one else who had such an extensive list of both underground and notorious connections built up from half a decade of living life on the edge.

Most of all – and this is what Karl Nummert had understood when Arno was first appointed to the position – nobody else had such few allegiances. Even at the age of twenty-five, Arno Hiller was embittered enough to see that everyone around him could be a threat. He'd seen enough to know that a fundamental truth lay in the idea that to trust completely *in anything* was a fool's mistake, and in this day and age that was no small advantage.

And it mattered. For the wise-heads at the Kriminalpolizei knew the increasing relevance of hiring people who had no faith in one cause or another. There were enough fascists on their way into government, and enough Communists on their way out, to make public life an unbalanced affair as it was. And if these new recruits happened to be young men who could be easily shaped into avid servants of Kripo, then so much so the better. Rather that than the grizzled veterans who still harboured bitterness over the war, who never did as they were told and who stuck fast to their own political affiliations when it was better to have none.

Besides which, changes were ahead. Everyone knew it. A change in the country's leadership always brought with it reforms of some sort; with Hitler, the changes were bound to be more sweeping. The men at Kripo simply didn't know what those changes would amount to yet. Rumours suggested that the criminal police would fall under the control of the SS Protection Squadron. Others said that it would become militarised and used as a metropolitan army. And nobody had any faith that the small Jewish contingent of the force would last in their posts very long.

In all these respects, Arno Hiller emerged as an ideal initiate. Young but with experience behind him. Determined without having a cause to fight, and disaffected enough to get himself into trouble without thinking twice of the consequences.

After dropping off the petrol canister and registration plate at police headquarters, Arno arranged to meet an old friend at Aschinger's restaurant just around the corner. He took the knife with him, knowing his contact would undoubtedly have something to say about it.

Lovis Blume was a reliable sort. Arno had first met him when he was mixed up with the criminal gangs of Berlin. Dealers, importers, racketeers, these criminals were never short of a job if you asked around. Mostly the work involved transporting packages across the city from one mob to another. Cocaine, weapons – whatever contraband was running at the time. They never told you what was inside the package, but by the way they checked you over, you could often guess how much it was worth.

It had been a long time since Arno had been a transporter for the gangs – he gave that up when he first met Monika – but he made a point of not completely burning his bridges with some of his closer associates. Before his current position it was a matter of insurance, a way of keeping a foot in the door in case of a rainy day. Now he didn't need the work but the contacts were no less useful to him.

He and Blume had first become friends inside the network known as *Libelle* (Dragonfly), whose members wore gold signet rings and were bound to absolute secrecy before the police. Arno knew that Blume still had his wise head and wouldn't stick too closely to the code. Some people have that way about them. They acquire an astute mind and they keep it, even in the rough-edged setting of the criminal underworld. While everyone else was hustling and getting into arguments, Blume did his own thing and kept to his own pace, which was as steady and deliberate as honey sliding from a spoon.

Arno approached the restaurant. Its square windows were lit up with lines of glowing bulbs like a row of stage lights. Inside, Blume was sat at the back, chatting to a waiter who wore a crisp white jacket and was smiling at a joke Blume had just made.

Another waiter, a grizzled walrus in a grimy-white coat, came to greet Arno at the door. He took him through the restaurant to Blume's table. Aschinger's was a popular hang-out for the young middle-classes, those city employees who worked as clerks and typists by day and liked to feel it was all worth it by night. The main attraction was the price: Aschinger's was cheap enough to eat a three-course meal for under five marks a head.

Arno took a seat at the table opposite Blume, who was eating from a great bowl of turtle soup into which he dunked bread rolls and tore off the sodden ends with his teeth.

'Sixty pfennigs!' Blume said by way of a greeting. He had a long face and big grey eyes, like an old horse. 'Always a bargain. Sixty pfennigs for a bowl of soup and as much bread as you can eat. There's no place like it in town.'

Arno ordered a plate of pickled herring and sour cream, with a glass of beer on the side.

'You should've had the soup,' Blume insisted as he ordered his second basket of warm bread. 'The bread never runs out.'

Blume was one of those gang members who never quite seemed to fit into any one mob or other – and had the scars to prove it. His face was so riven with nooks and slashes it looked as though it might fall apart at any moment. His main occupation was as a thief but he was also something of an expert in weapons too, and knew how to procure just about any drug you might care to ask for. He was a certain type of hardened criminal: calm, utterly indifferent, and more intelligent than most. He seemed neither to have dreams nor fears. On a good day, he could pack hefty takings from his work as a fingersmith, no problem.

And he always wore a tie. Not just any old tie, but a narrow leather tie that was brown and grimy and every year darkened by a shade from never being washed. It was now almost black.

'If I spend sixty pfennigs here, I'll have four marks to spend at Sing-Sing later. There's a nice looking redhead I've got my eye on there.'

Arno sat back in his chair, waiting for his beer to arrive.

'How are you enjoying yourself, then?' Blume asked, chewing through a ball of bread as he spoke.

Arno looked at him quizzically.

'Or should I say, *detective*?'

'Oh, yes. Good. It doesn't change anything, between us of course,' Arno replied. Code of honour meant that he would never use his new position to get Blume into trouble.

'So what did you want to see me about?'

Arno leaned forward.

'A car was found. Out in the southwest quarter, halfway to Potsdam. There was a dead body inside. The whole thing had been completely torched, nothing left but embers. At the moment there isn't anything to identify the victim except the car registration. I'm looking into that as we speak. Anything you've got, anything you've heard, could be useful.'

'The make of the car?'

'Don't know yet.'

'Anything unusual?'

'Unusual? Apart from a dead body inside a car?'

'I've seen stranger things than that,' Blume said, taking a glug of beer.

'Maybe you can help with this?' Arno slipped his hand into his jacket, looked around and discreetly took out the knife. He placed it on the table and coolly laid his napkin on top. He pushed it across to Blume, who took it under the table to inspect.

'Fine blade,' he said. 'Made by Aesculap. Solid nickel crossguard. The ivory grip will clean up nicely – I take it you found this in the wreckage?'

Arno nodded.

Blume now dipped his head to look again. His interest in weaponry was obsessive, which made him a good source of information.

'There are words etched into the blade.'

'Yes.'

'*All for Germany*, it says. They've been scorched by the fire but you can just about make them out. This is a Nazi knife. Just here, on the grip, you can see the Nazi *Reichsadler* – the eagle crest. The blade would have come with a scabbard originally. More of a showpiece than a weapon. I've seen Stormtroopers carrying them. It's all about honourable membership, fraternity, that sort of thing. They love that kind of symbolism.'

'You mean it's ceremonial as opposed to a real knife?'

'Don't get me wrong, you could still do plenty of damage with it, no trouble at all. It's just not its main purpose.'

Blume pushed the knife back across the table and promptly mopped up the last of his soup. He used his leather tie to dab the corners of his mouth, then crossed his arms over his chest, apparently satisfied that he'd eaten enough.

'Anything else?' Blume asked.

Arno considered. 'The question is, did it belong to the corpse inside the car or to someone else? And is it a murder weapon?'

'And your job is to find out,' Blume surmised.

Arno picked up the knife with the napkin still over it and slipped it back into his pocket. The restaurant around him was filling up with evening diners, all shades of young folk out for the night. The atmosphere was upbeat and happy. He thought to himself how rare it was to find a corner of Berlin that still felt free and relaxed. He remembered how he used to live for these places, where people revelled in cosmopolitan living, where young women and men flirted with each other with liberal abandon. A few years ago, the whole of the city was like this.

Just then, two Nazi Stormtroopers came in and the atmosphere shifted in an instant.

10

The Nazis' rubber capes sparkled with what looked like jewels of icy rainwater. They shook themselves off like dogs emerging from a river and left a trail of water as they crossed the restaurant floor. They had about them a bold, uncompromising air, as if they had grown accustomed to getting their own way and expected it. They ordered two dinners before they picked a place to settle, arrogantly rearranging the furniture so they would have somewhere to put their feet up. Their sinister black boots had shiny metal clips, which they unfastened and loosened, stretching out across several chairs. Pools of water collected under them as they dripped dry.

The whole restaurant was aware of their presence, the way they barked orders at the waiters and talked loudly so everyone else could hear. Their confident voices grated against Arno's ears. He looked at Blume, who was certainly no supporter of the Nazis either. Blume's eyes narrowed. Arno half swivelled around watching their loutish behaviour. When he turned to face Blume again, he found he'd left the table and was silently departing through the front door.

Arno stayed and kept a low profile. After a few minutes, one of the Nazis began to get agitated. He'd noticed that the restaurant had failed to put up a red flag. He said that with Hitler's appointment as Chancellor, the

60

swastika flag was an important sign of allegiance. The other Stormtrooper firmly agreed with him, at which the first officer got to his feet and demanded to see whoever was in charge.

The proprietor of the restaurant was summoned. She came up from a set of cellar steps. She was a short, round woman with a glossy ochre face like an old varnished oil painting. The Nazi loomed over her and demanded to know why there was no flag, and by implication, no recognition of the new leadership.

'Is this a Yiddish establishment?' he challenged bitterly. 'What are you, a servant of the Jews?'

'Where is the flag?' the other Nazi insisted, getting to his feet.

The manager had a stern, frozen look. She was either unmoved by their demands or else too frightened to say a word. After a short exchange, she quietly went to a drawer behind the counter and unfolded a large Nazi flag. The officer was only partially satisfied. He took the flag from her and impatiently went around the restaurant looking for a place to hang it. He eventually settled on a bookcase in the corner, where he removed two books and used them as weights to hold the hanging flag in place.

Arno was listening from his table at the back of the room. He kept his face turned and his eyes lowered. He didn't recognise the two Brownshirts but that didn't mean they wouldn't recognise him. His history with the Nazi Party was a messy one. More than anyone, he knew what a band of despots was really being shoe-horned into the Reichstag. Some people said that the reputation of Hilter and his cronies was unfair. 'Nothing but a rumour,' one person said to him recently. 'They're here to run the country, to support the nation's people.'

But Arno thought otherwise. It wasn't hard to notice

61

the repugnant cartoons on the front pages of the Nazi newspapers. And how come the David stars had begun appearing on the windows of the Jewish shopfronts? It was coming – *something* was coming – he could feel it. Those who defended Hitler seemed to overlook the fact that Berlin had turned into a cauldron of anger and anxiety ready to bubble over at any moment. They didn't mention how every time an election drew near you'd see more and more Nazi Brownshirts, *Kommunistische Partei Deutschlands* and Social Democratic *Reichsbanner* members, clashing in the streets with the same result in the end.

Violence broke out. Bottles were thrown, or if not bottles then chairs and table-legs; whatever they could lay their hands on would become weapons to haul at their enemies. As the heat was turned up, knives and clubs, then brass knuckles and guns. When people died – which they did at a rate that most people were unwilling to admit – then they were deemed 'martyrs' by those on their own side, and 'enemies of the state' by those who opposed them. It was all a nasty game. The trouble was, it was a game many found tempting to take part in.

Of more pressing concern was the fact that Arno once paraded as a member of the Party himself. To turn your back on a movement like that can end up becoming a deadly mistake. The last thing he wanted was to be questioned by two soldiers drunk on power and for him to inform them who he worked for.

He decided it was time to leave the scene, so he slipped away from his chair and skirted around the side of the restaurant. He went to reach the street door unnoticed, but a voice rang out in his direction before he got to it. Then one of the Nazis jumped behind him and Arno felt himself being hooked by the arm and spun towards the bookcase where the flag hung.

'Salute it,' the Nazi ordered.

'Why?' Arno questioned as he pulled himself free from the Nazi's grip.

'Everyone must salute it,' the Nazi partner said. 'Everyone in this restaurant.'

Arno frowned. He looked at the two soldiers and saw their excited young faces flushed with a sense of righteousness.

'Hail the flag,' the first soldier repeated.

'What are you, a peasant Communist? Salute it!'

Arno did nothing. He was in no mood for this. These men had no idea who he was, had no idea the degree of contempt he felt for them. There was no way he was going to salute the flag. It was more likely he would punch both of them in the face than raise his arm in the air.

'What is your name?' the Nazi asked.

Arno felt like putting these two in their place. He was a police detective after all. What power had he in circumstances like this? Perhaps he had none. Did it matter? The rules were changing on a daily basis, and these pair of brutes were unlikely to care.

'Who are you? Tell us or we will have to force you to tell us,' the Nazi went on. Arno noticed the Nazi had his hand on his baton, ready to brandish it.

'That's none of your business.'

'Salute the flag and say your name as you do so.'

'I will not.'

The Nazis took hold of Arno's left arm and braced it behind his back. The other grabbed his right arm and tussled to extend it upwards. They were strong and unrelenting, and Arno could feel his own strength being challenged.

Yet he resisted. He was not going to salute the flag. He'd spent too long hating that retched symbol to begin saluting it now. How long can a man stay silent? At a

63

certain point, enough is enough. Sooner or later, you have to say 'No.'

Then he remembered the knife in his pocket. He thought for a moment about using it – a quick slice through the abdomen would soon shut the Brownshirt up – but he knew it would spell more trouble for him if he did.

The eyes of all the restaurant were on him now, waiting for him to succumb and lift his arm – or else receive the beating he would surely get if he didn't. They stared with blank faces, wondering if they would be next to be made to stand in front of the flag. Would the Brownshirts go one by one around the room and force everyone to make the same stupid pledge?

With the hands of the two men on him, Arno had little choice but to give in. But he wasn't finished. He relaxed his arm and let them point it towards the ceiling; and yet as he did so, he turned his head and whispered something into one of the men's ears.

'What did you say?' the Brownshirt rebuked.

Arno gave a toothy grin.

'Say that again,' the Nazi snarled.

Arno repeated his words, only louder this time. 'You're afraid of not being taken seriously,' he stated. And then louder still: 'Scared witless, aren't you?'

Then he turned to the other Brownshirt and said, 'And you were bullied at school – now you've become the bully.'

He looked back to the first one. 'I'm right, aren't I? That's why you stamp your feet and shout. You're a quivering baby inside.'

The Brownshirts glared at each other dumbfounded. Their momentary pause told Arno that he'd hit a nerve with both of them. It was an old trick he learned from someone in the Dragonfly gang. Imply a weakness and it can disarm anyone – for a few seconds at least.

A few seconds was all he needed. He abruptly stood to attention and in a manner that was too peacockish to be anything other than sarcastic, shouted 'My name is…' Then he swiped a glass tankard from one of the tables and smashed it onto one of the Nazi's jaws before swiftly launching his sharpened elbow into the stomach of the other. Both soldiers lurched backwards as a spray of blood rose in the air. Without hesitation, Arno left the premises. He raised his collar and walked briskly into the night-time street. He raced down the avenue and disappeared along an alley as he felt his adrenaline rush through him.

He hadn't outgrown the pleasure of dancing on the edge of danger. He might have taken out his beer-token police badge and pulled rank on those two. But then they'd still expect him to salute the flag. No, it was better this way: surprise them with bare-faced bluster. He laughed to himself as he dispersed into the city night. Well, he wasn't the first Berliner to throw a punch at a Brownshirt.

Later, he found himself walking to Wilmersdorf district where Monika used to live. His encounter with the two Nazis had stirred memories of her. He walked beside the grand three-story townhouses with their stout timber doors and lace curtains shimmering over the windows. In one window stood a bust of Beethoven glowering into the street. At another, a large ginger cat lay sprawled out, its eyes wide and green. Streetlamps filtered through and shone into the front rooms, where nurses soothed babies and old men sat in armchairs reading newspapers.

He felt an urgent craving to live as these people must, in their grand homes with a placid, luxurious sense of fate – not his own twisted, unsettled existence.

65

Most of all, he missed Monika. The life he had begun to dream of before the eve of her departure was still fixed in his memory. Where was she now? Was she stood at a window looking out over an American street, thinking of him? He looked up at the faint suggestion of stars twinkling and wondered if she could see the same constellations arcing across the sky.

11

Come the new day, Arno let his mind crawl over the particulars of the case. He thought about the knife and the lonely landscape where the burnt-out car had been found. It seemed such a savage way to die, cremated on an expanse of wasteland with nobody there to witness it. He began to wonder if one of his duties over the next few days might be to visit the victim's family once the body had been identified.

Just then, he heard knocking on his apartment door. A visitor, at this time of the morning? When he opened it, he found his brother-in-law standing on the doorstep.

Thomas Strack was married to his sister. Arno assumed he had come to pick up the suitcase borrowed for the move.

'Come on in,' Arno said with a wave of indifference. To Arno, Thomas was one of those men who let life rule over him and was too much of a stickler for convention to do anything about it. In all the time they'd known each other, they had never quite crossed the line into mutual friendship, probably because their temperaments were just so different. One was like the modern kino on the Kurfürstendamm, the other like the traditional Wintergarten Theatre in Berlin-Mitte.

'I hope I'm not interrupting,' Thomas said as he stepped inside.

'The suitcase is just through here.'

'Suitcase? Oh, I haven't come for that. I'm here to ask for a favour, in actual fact.' Thomas began to unfasten the belt on his khaki raincoat. 'I'll get to the point. I know you're busy.'

'Go on.' Arno led the way through to the kitchenette.

'This is an improvement,' Thomas said, commenting on the apartment as he glanced around. 'I mean, compared to your last one. Your sister will be pleased.'

'What can I do for you?'

'Well, the thing is, I've been asked to write a piece for the *Frankfurter Zeitung*. It'll be all about the scene in Berlin at the start of the new year. Think of it as a report from the front line.'

'You're writing for a newspaper?'

'Yes, I've been commissioned to write an article.' Thomas grinned. He was proud of his announcement and he didn't mind showing it. It was something he'd been working on privately for several years. Now finally he'd won his first significant commission and he wanted to bask in its sunshine.

'I'm on their books as a freelancer. Up until now, I've had a few small bylines in the *Börsen-Courier*, but now I've got a bigger stage.'

'Good for you,' Arno said. He couldn't help but envy Thomas. It began and ended with the fact that his brother-in-law was unnaturally wealthy. Moreover, it was inherited wealth and that just made it worse. 'If you don't need to work for a living,' Arno responded, 'then I suppose you can do whatever you want with your time.'

'This is my way of making a living,' Thomas said, hoping it sufficed as an explanation.

'And where do I fit in?'

'I'm sketching a portrait of our age and I thought you may be able to help. The theme of the feature is the underbelly of Berlin. They want me to write about the criminal gangs, the seedier side if you will. I thought that since you are a detective now I could interview you. We could talk about the crimes you've solved and the criminals you've arrested.'

Arno ran his hand through his hair. The proposition suddenly took on a different hue, one that could be to his advantage. Maybe news of the incident would be a good opportunity to call for witnesses or information that could help.

'What exactly do you want to know?'

'Do you have time right now?'

'Why not?'

'Wonderful.' Thomas took out a small notebook and a pencil. 'Why don't you start with the job you're working on right now?'

Arno cleared his throat. Thomas was already scribbling with his pencil even before he'd said a word.

'I've just been assigned to a new case. Two days ago a burnt-out motorcar was found, out in the industrial south-west. What makes it interesting is that there was a dead body inside.'

'A murder?'

'Actually, we don't know that. The victim is yet to be identified. They're complete charcoal from head to toe, but off the record it looks to me like it was deliberate.'

'A political assassination?' Thomas said, his voice jumping in excitement.

'What makes you say that?'

'Oh nothing. Just that – well, it wouldn't be the first dead body to turn up with a political motivation behind it.'

Arno paused. He thought about the knife he'd found in the wreckage, which presently rested in a drawer in his kitchenette. Could Thomas be right? He decided to keep the detail of the knife to himself.

'Let's not jump to conclusions. Do you know how many homicides we get across our desks?' he said back with a deliberate helping of condescension.

'How many?'

'Dozens every day. And most of them are little more than domestic squabbles that get out of hand. A husband loses his temper and goes too far. Or it can be the other way around. Women can be just as bloodthirsty, let me tell you.'

Thomas began scribbling in his notebook. Arno watched on. He wanted to sound wise and jaded, but in truth he had no idea how many dead bodies turned up in Berlin. Still, he liked it that Thomas was hanging onto his every word.

'But in this particular case you suspect murder?' Thomas said, rattling his pencil inside his teeth.

'We found a petrol canister nearby. That's what we're focusing on.'

'Petrol? You think someone doused the car and set it alight – with the person inside it?'

'Slow down. It's too early to say.' Arno wandered over to the window and peered across through to the dense tree branches of the nearby park. 'The worse thing we can do is make reflex judgements.'

'I'd like to see the car, if I can,' Thomas then said. 'Will you take me with you when you go next?'

'I don't know,' Arno said ambivalently.

'I would be extremely grateful.'

'Well,' Arno replied slowly, 'what harm can it do.'

12

The temperature had lifted by a few degrees. Instead of snow, the streets were now daubed in mounds of brown slush. The two men rode on Arno's motorbike, with Thomas sitting upright, his arms braced behind his back holding onto the rear. The exhaust fumes left a long white tail hanging in the air.

At the edge of the city, they found the dirt track and turned in. With the snow thawing, the rear wheels of the motorbike slipped into the buttery ruts, forcing them to hold their balance as the bike dipped and bobbed. Up ahead, the car wreck was steadily disintegrating into something that resembled a great black anthill.

'As you can see, a large proportion was consumed in the flames,' Arno said. By now the body had been removed by the coroner and it was clear that shovels had been employed to gather up the remains.

'It's shocking to think someone was in there,' Thomas said. Now that they were at the site it was obvious he was a bit edgy.

As for Arno, he was feeling pleased. 'I wanted to examine things on my own without the local police leering over my every move,' he said crouching at the wreck.

Thomas stood for a moment and glanced around at the wider setting. The open fields stretched beyond a wire fence, reaching a border of trees in three directions. In the west, a factory spurted smoke into the sky, lit white by the brilliant winter sun.

'Do you know where we are?' Arno asked.

'Broadly,' Thomas said squinting.

'That's the locomotive factory over there.'

'Orenstein and Koppel?'

'That's right.'

'Yes, I remember.' Thomas had been here years before in different circumstances. 'Mind if I take a photograph?' he asked, purposefully shifting his thoughts on. He began trampling through the long grasses to get a wider shot, making his way to the wire fence.

As Thomas fiddled with his camera, Arno toured the burnt-out car and did his best to work out where his investigation should continue. It was at moments like this that he wished he had some of the official training behind him, thinking he should have cordoned off the area to establish the scene of the crime. And now Thomas was here with him taking photographs and trampling over potential evidence.

'Better stick with me,' he called over to Thomas, waving him back. Then he thought about what he had discovered so far: the petrol canister, the knife, the car registration plate. But where did the evidence begin and end? The petrol can, for instance: it was highly probable it belonged to this crime, but if so why not conceal the evidence better? Whether the can belonged to the person in the car or an arsonist, why dispose of it in the woods?

Just then he heard Thomas call out. 'I found something.' He was stood beside the fence up to his knees in dew sodden grass, with his eyes fixed as he looked down.

'Hold on, I'm coming,' Arno said, rolling up his sleeves.

Thomas was stood pointing to a pool of water whose surface had frozen over. On the near edge, something was protruding from the ice.

Arno pulled back the grass as he began skirting over the frosty crust of the pond. The ice beneath his feet began to crunch and crack under his weight. He bent down to reach forward, and at full stretch just managed to wrap his fingers around the jutting form. Giving it a twist and a wrench, he fished the object out of the water. There they found themselves looking at a square block of wood with a protruding circle jagged with splinters. Arno pulled back from the water and raised himself tall.

'This area should have been searched,' he said as he turned the object over in his hands.

'Do you think it's related?' Thomas asked.

Arno considered the possibility. It was obviously a man-made object, but what it was exactly he couldn't say. Just the fact that it was there made him think, 'Why wasn't this picked up before?' He wondered how long it had been there? If it had been in the pond all along, then it was likely that the two local police officers had done a sloppy job scouting the scene. And that told Arno only one thing: that nobody really took the crime scene seriously. They all thought it was an open-and-shut accident – to be assigned, therefore, to someone who wasn't ready for a genuine murder case.

'I'll take this with me,' Arno said. He looked at the block again. The wood was damp and partly fractured. It could be nothing. Then again, it could have another story.

'Where was the petrol can found?' Thomas asked.

'Over in that direction. About a ten minute walk.'

'Can you show me?'

They made their way over the creamy mud track down into the thicket of trees where the shadows made the air cooler and the green of the ivy leaves and brambles darkened. The air seemed more silent inside the woods, as if the emptiness of the land was more palpable in this more intimate setting. A rustle in the bushes or a bird singing were the only noises for miles around.

They went to the spot where Arno had picked up the canister. Thomas took out his notebook and started scribbling away. Meanwhile, Arno went on further, down the sloping path that turned into a winding track beneath the archway of a tree bough. He didn't come this far before and realised that the network of wooded pathways was far more extensive than he first thought. As he turned, the winter sunlight streamed in and lit up an immense cloud of swarming gnats. He waved his way through the insects, keeping his eyes alive to the possibility of another clue.

Walking this desolate track felt a thousand miles from the stone forest of Berlin. He stood silent for a moment and let the wild glare of the sun dazzle his eyes. In these cold months, when the sun barely lifted above the treetops, it was a pleasure to feel its heat on his face. The earth around him was a twist of wiry brambles and holly bushes, along with numerous tree stumps amputated for firewood. The path seemed to go on and on, so he kept a mental track of his whereabouts.

After a few minutes, he began to hear Thomas call after him with what he detected as a touch of concern in Thomas' voice. This was where a murder suspect could have come, perhaps even the path he might have taken to escape. To be moving out alone here, among the sharp rays of sunlight and the dark shadows it painted, could be risky. And as these thoughts passed through Arno's mind, he began to feel the power of the idea, as a twisted tree trunk presented the form of his culprit.

Now Thomas' calls fell quiet and it suddenly seemed like each turn in the path could reveal something unexpected. A flock of crows then broke out into a racket, circling madly up above. Arno stopped and paused. He looked back and saw nothing. Tree branches creaked from the warmth of the sun. Mist rose up from the wood. Then there was the sound of water trickling somewhere.

At that very moment, he became aware he was being watched. He moved into where the overgrowth was thicker, then he dipped behind a large bush with white berries. Ahead of him, an oak tree had a rope swing tied to it. It had a loop tied in the end and looked for all the world like a noose hanging from the gallows.

He scrambled through the underwood and arrived where it opened into a clearing. The grasses here were crisscrossed by the rutted tracks made by wild animals; hares, boars and badgers. Then in the corner of his eye, he saw a figure moving in the trees. He hunkered down among the grass and just at the edge of the opening he saw the stranger again. There was someone there with him.

He moved towards the shadow, traversing the slippery ground beneath his feet where a carpet of decaying orange coloured leaves covered the floor. Then behind him, he heard something snap.

He turned and was caught by the blaze of the sun. He shaded his eyes.

'Who's there?' he shouted.

The sound of breaking tree branches seemed to circle around him. He turned and turned again.

'Come out. Show yourself.'

The calm of the wood was broken like a crack through a mirror. Instinct took him in the direction of the dirt track. He remained cautious over the slippery clay, whilst his fists were clenched in readiness. He clambered up through a tangled blur of coppice and wildwood. The brambles snagged on his trousers and the thorns of dog-rose caught on his coat. The flock of black crows swept overhead, cawing wildly.

Finally, the horizontal of the track came into view. As he emerged, he saw Thomas there with his camera stood silhouetted against the strong sunlight like a statue.

Back on firm ground, the sense of alarm began to slip away as he felt the mysterious presence disappear.

'Are you okay?' Thomas said. 'You look tense.'

'Don't worry, I'm fine.'

'Did you see anything?'

Arno shook his head. Then turning, he said, 'How long before you can get those photographs developed? I want to see everything you have captured today.'

13

Arno and Thomas returned to the police headquarters on Alexanderplatz. Arno's office was a large draughty room with wood panels across the ceiling and an enormous clay stove in the corner. In winter, the stove had to be restocked with coal every morning to stop it from going out. His desk was antique, riddled with woodworm and burnished bronze by the thousand hands that had been there before him. His chair had a broken spring beneath the leather seat and his typewriter jammed constantly. But above all, Arno was obliged to share the office with someone else.

Bernard Hölz was young and intense and had the eager arrogance of someone expecting to succeed – whatever it might take. He had joined the agency at the same time as Arno, but unlike Arno, he'd been through the official training route. A methodical, scientific type, he never let Arno forget the fact that their careers were so contrasting. Hölz was also an ardent supporter of Hitler and did little to hide the fact. He saw his job as a moral one as much as a practical affair: cleaning up the streets of Berlin was more than just a job; it was a duty.

Thomas was still trailing Arno as they entered the office and came across Hölz sitting at the desk they shared. He was laying out a deck of playing cards. His hair was trimmed in straight lines across his forehead and

77

he smelled strongly of pickled cabbage – which he ate rigorously for its health benefits.

'What are you doing?' Arno said abruptly. He always made a point of never cowering to his colleague.

'*Guten tag*,' Hölz replied, refusing to look up.

Arno took off his coat and hung it on the stand. As he did, he happened to knock Hölz's wide-brimmed hat onto the floor.

'I need the desk back,' Arno said.

'Our desk,' Hölz corrected as he laid out another playing card. Eventually, he raised his eyes. 'Who is this?' he said, glancing at Thomas.

'This is an associate of mine,' Arno replied, choosing to leave out the fact that Thomas was his brother-in-law and an aspiring journalist. 'He's assisting me – he has specialist insight.'

Thomas stepped forward and shook Hölz by the hand. 'I'm working for the *Frankfurter Zeitung*,' He stated proudly. 'I'm writing a piece on the criminal underbelly of Berlin.'

Arno frowned.

'Are you now?' Hölz widened his eyes with a cruel sort of delight. 'A journalist? I must be careful about what I say in that case.'

Arno stepped in. 'Thomas, let me introduce you to Bernard Hölz. He's everybody's idea of a perfect student. He's never late and his shoes are always polished. He won a gold medal at the training college. A genuine star pupil. And what he doesn't know about sauerkraut is not worth knowing. He also likes to play cards – apparently.'

'Oh, I'm not playing,' Hölz retorted. 'I'm deliberating. My brain, you see, enjoys being prompted in the most unusual ways. I'm rare like that. I do some of my best thinking when I'm asleep, for instance. Laying out cards like this is not dissimilar to the Chinese *I Ching*, which I've no doubt you've never heard of.'

'It looks to me like you're playing solitaire,' Arno replied. 'Badly.'

Arno took his seat across the desk from Hölz and began unpacking his bag. He wished Hölz was out today. He was everything Arno regarded as irritating: methodical, patient and tediously rule-bound. What made him all the more unbearable was his unshakable confidence. He may have been clever, but his conceitedness made him impossible to respect. And all these playing cards on the table was just a feeble performance meant to give the impression of mental prowess.

'The Chinese *I Ching*?' Thomas picked up. 'The ancient art of divination, if I'm not mistaken.'

'You two can keep your Chinese superstition.'

'Actually, it's not superstition. The principle of the *I Ching* is that…'

'I don't care,' Arno interrupted. 'Besides, we haven't got time to talk hocus-pocus with Hölz. Come with me. I want to see if they've traced the car registration yet.'

Thomas gave a grin. 'Great. I'm coming.'

'How is the investigation going?' Hölz called after them. 'I've heard you've been given a genuine case to work on?'

'You don't need to concern yourself about that.' He knew Hölz was trying to needle him.

'I heard you found a body in a car?'

'We have work to do,' Arno replied. He pulled on Thomas' arm. 'Come on.'

Thomas looked back. He was intrigued by Hölz. Unlike Arno, he appreciated someone who took a disciplined approach to their work and who dressed for the part. It surprised him, therefore, to notice the state of Hölz's shoes beneath the desk: that they were caked in mud.

They left the office and went together to a row of telephone booths at the other end of the building. Arno spoke to the exchange and was put through to the appropriate department.

Thomas watched stricken with interest as he waited for news on the car's owner. Ever since inheriting a sum of money five years before, he'd found himself surprisingly set adrift from purpose, not at all free from life's worries as he imagined such a sum of money would allow him. But now, in the tumult of the present moment, he felt he had returned to the real world of activity, grit and enterprise. Finally, perhaps, in the restless occupation of conjecture and speculation that is the writer's lot, he had found his vocation.

Eventually, Arno put down the receiver and turned to face Thomas. He had grown pale and had that far away look in his eyes that seemed to beg a question.

'What is it? Did they tell you who the car belonged to?'

'Yes.'

'Who?'

'The name they gave me – it's hard to credit – they told me the car belonged to – Erich Ostwald.'

'Erich?'

'The car was registered in 1931. A black Adler saloon.'

'Erich? Are you sure?'

'He was the last registered owner of the car.'

'Erich Ostwald, my old friend. How can that be?'

'I don't know, but time will tell.'

PART III

14

In the dim setting of a hotel room, Erich Ostwald woke up with a gasp. He sat upright and felt a sudden ache in his side, at which he lifted his shirt to reveal several bruised ribs from the fight with Mayer. He turned over to relieve the pain and lay back down again to press his head against the pillow.

Remarkably, he'd been able to sleep for a few hours. Though it was a dreamless sleep, a complete blackout of consciousness for which he felt grateful. Still, something else was weighing on him, not just the pain pressing into his ribcage but some graver issue that aggravated him.

The undue haste with which he left the blazing car meant things hadn't gone exactly to plan. He hadn't covered all his tracks. Somewhere in that desolate stretch of land was the evidence that had been his most important duty to destroy. The mallet. The precise reason he had chosen a weapon made of wood was so it could be discarded on the bonfire. But the unknown vehicle that suddenly appeared on the horizon had derailed him and had forced him to dispose of it otherwise.

It was the mallet head that puzzled him the most. Perhaps it would remain submerged in the water where he'd thrown it, at least until springtime when the pond might dry up. He couldn't be sure, and that lack of certainty weighed on his mind.

If it was found, maybe it would be mistaken for the object used to kill Erich Ostwald? In that case, then it didn't matter. It would be treated as yet another piece of evidence in favour of the story he wished to create. As long as there was no trace of Mayer on it then there wasn't a problem. But if the police did find any link to Mayer, then the case could get complicated.

The police needed to conclude that it was Erich Ostwald inside the car – the tragic casualty of an accident or perhaps the victim of a murder. Either way, the investigation would dredge up files from the basements of the police archives and a picture of the victim steadily pieced together. It wouldn't take too long for the cross-references to be made and for the inevitable blanks to be filled in. They would discover a man whose history was cut through with split allegiances. Finally, his work for the *Abwehr* would be uncovered, and hence a picture of a defector would emerge. From then, the second alternative would become the only sensible conclusion. *A political murder.*

Whichever of these two conclusions they chose to arrive at, they both depended on the first principle that it was *Erich Ostwald* inside the car. And for now, there was nothing else for it but to push on with his plan…

He rolled over in bed and felt the sting of his ribs electrify his whole left side as he got up. His hotel was on the far reaches of Berlin's southern edge, just beyond Tempelhof airport, which could be another escape route if he needed it. He was staying in room number 211. It had a broken mirror and a gas-lamp hanging from the ceiling covered with an orange glass shade. The room glowed like a tangerine when it was lit. The bed was an iron frame, the mattress heavy, hard and covered in

84

stains. A gas stove with a slot for coins stood in the corner. When he dropped a coin in it, nothing happened.

The hotel itself was ageing and worn, and smelled of coffee and turnips, or possibly coffee made from turnips. He'd used a fake name when checking in and also made a point of never lingering in the lobby. He always came in through a side entrance which meant he could reach the staircase to the second floor more directly. The hotel's newly installed communication system was also an advantage: every room was fitted with a Bakelite bell-push which, once pressed, would illuminate a light above the reception. A flickering matrix of green lights pulsed on and off that had the uninitiated staff running around in circles but meant he could remain relatively unseen.

He requested a cafetière of coffee and the latest newspaper to be left outside his room. Much of the paper's front page concerned the appointment of the new chancellor and what it would mean for the make-up of the Reichstag. There was speculation over the political futures of Papen and Hindenburg, and whether or not Hitler would call for one further election to secure his party's position.

Erich read it all in a vague manner. He had no energy to think about politics. The only thing he cared about was if his crime had been reported yet. He licked his fingers and passed through the pages of the paper but found no mention of the burnt-out car. It was a relief in some way. But sooner or later the news would come out, and that would mean a whole different set of forces to contend with.

Then he began to imagine what would be said *when* the story appeared. The headlines would begin with sensationalism: '*Prominent Berliner from Ostwald family found in exploded motorcar.*' After that, as the days and weeks passed, a more factual slant: '*Wreckage suggests tragic accident'* or *'Political murder induced by fire.'*

He stood up and went over to the cracked mirror. As he ran his hands through his bronze crest of hair, he considered the next stage of his disappearance. From his bag he pulled out a sharp razor blade and started to cut his hair. He was soon pulling thick tufts from his head, leaving behind a sparse mess with bare skin showing through in patches. He looked botched, which was more or less the effect he was after.

Next, he pressed the electric bell-push. When an errand boy came, Erich put a hat on to hide his hair and asked, 'Where is the nearest chemist?'

'There's one at the far end of the street, sir.' The boy checked his watch. 'You should just make it before it closes for lunch.'

Erich tipped the boy, then went from the hotel to the apothecary at the end of the road. He purchased a bottle of hair dye, then promptly returned to the hotel. At the sink he half stripped off before covering his hair in the dye. It was as black as boot polish.

Next, he shaved off his moustache and beard. He took off his clothes and dressed himself in a dark suit he'd brought with him. He took the sheet from his bed and made a sack out of it by tying knots into the opposite corners. Into this sack he pushed the bundle of his old clothes; come nightfall he would make his way to the rear of the hotel where the Landwehr Canal ran within twenty yards, and by adding armfuls of rubble, would send the sack to the bottom of the murky waterway.

Finally, he put on a pair of horn-rimmed glasses to complete his look. Without his hat, he ventured into the lobby to find the same bellboy. The lad looked at him vaguely and asked if he was looking for a room. Erich was pleased. The disguise seemed to be a success.

Erich knew the Excelsior Hotel well. Many years before he used it to meet up with his fiancée, where they would stay for days at a time in the lap of luxury. He remembered how they would step out from their taxi straight under the canopy of the hotel entrance, then in through the revolving doors of the lobby. Lines of bellboys would be there, wearing caps and uniforms with brass buttons running up their chests, waiting to serve. Erich would have a twenty mark tip at the ready, and from that moment on, whichever bellboy received it would be eager to please all day long.

But that was another time in his life, when he was free and at liberty to play the role he always enjoyed: the libertine, the eccentric, the connoisseur.

Now he was here for a completely different purpose. As he entered, the scene was reminiscent of years gone by, with the music of a violin player in some distant room gliding through the air. The place gleamed with varnished wood, polished brass, and the scent of cologne worn by the wealthy women who came to stay there.

Erich clutched Mayer's room key in his pocket, which was attached to a metal tag with the number 417 etched in. It was a risk being here. Luckily it was busy inside, mainly with guests coming down for afternoon coffee. The restaurant was wood-panelled with gleaming floors and long rugs running between the tables. Chandeliers with a hundred arms hung overhead and in the centre stood a marble statue of Diana the Huntress.

He took the marble staircase up to the fourth floor and made his way to room 417. After loitering for a moment he put his ear to the door. He knocked to be certain there was nobody inside before entering. In the room he found a large made-up bed with Mayer's work clothes tossed across it. Erich didn't plan to stay long.

87

He used the flap of his jacket like a glove to open one of the bedside drawers, then he took out a cheque from his wallet.

It was written out to Wolfgang Mayer, to the value of 4,000 marks. Several months before, Erich had lent on the services of an old acquaintance from his university days by the name of Albrecht Hodder. Erich remembered him as a talented pianist and an able rock climber. In normal times, he ran a print-works on Landsberger Strasse, yet ever since the market crash, he'd begun using his printing equipment to produce high-grade forged documents.

The cheque that Erich had procured bore the signatory of Count Hermann Graf von Hessen, the Nazi Gruppenführer of the Berlin SA. All Erich had to do was fill in the payee's name and thereby ensure his victim was seen to have received a bounty. And where would be better to plant the cheque other than in Mayer's hotel room? It would serve as evidence linking Mayer to his death, the payout for the murder. He placed it inside the drawer.

Before he left, he performed a quick inspection of the room and disturbed the bedclothes to make it look like the bed had been slept in. He found Mayer's tool bag under the bed, just as the city clocks struck three o'clock. It was time to go. Three minutes later he was moving down the marble staircase and making his way through the lobby. Then, as he approached the revolving doors he felt a tap on his shoulder. He turned around impassively, hoping that he hadn't been recognised.

Before him stood a man in military uniform, with a steel helmet and a rifle on his back. The stranger glanced at him up and down. Erich did the same and quickly identified the man as a member of the *Sicherheitspolizei* –

the anti-riot police that tended to stalk the streets looking for trouble-makers and any sign of weapons.

'Can I help you?' Erich asked.

'As a matter of fact, you can,' the policeman replied. He had a round face and bushy moustache. 'Everybody passing through here must identify themselves.'

'Expecting trouble?'

'There are reports of windows being smashed in a neighbouring hotel. Are you staying here?'

'Certainly.' Erich dangled the key for room 417 in the air.

'Very well, on your way then.'

Erich then dipped his head and passed through the revolving doors, out into the wintery afternoon.

15

Erich made his way back to his own hotel, considering his next steps. He couldn't abandon the idea that he had to do something about the mallet. If he could avoid it falling into the possession of the police then it needn't form part of their evidence haul. He just had to get his hands on the mallet head again.

As he strode through the busy streets, soaked in his thoughts, he suddenly caught hold of a woman who stumbled in front of him.

'Are you alright?' he asked.

The woman lifted her face from beneath her dark green beret and looked straight into Erich's eyes. She almost looked like a porcelain doll, ivory-skinned with large grey eyes, yet there was something familiar about her too. She was young with wavy red hair and dressed in a tweed trench coat.

'I am sorry. I just lost my footing.'

'That's okay,' Erich said, releasing her from his grip. He thought, 'That face, I've seen it before – but where?'

'Thank you, I'll be on my way now,' she said and walked off with a saunter.

Erich turned around to see her sink through the hustle and bustle of the street.

He reached his hotel and swiftly went up to his room. He'd picked up an afternoon edition of *Der Angriff*

90

and glanced over the front page. Being a Nazi paper its usual concern was with the evils of Communism, along with its perennial attacks on anyone whom it considered an enemy of true German interests. Today, however, the paper was celebrating the canonisation of Chancellor Hilter. Erich's eye drifted down the page and to his satisfaction, caught sight of his own name.

His burnt-out car had been found.

He read on eagerly. The article described how a body had been found and the vehicle's owner accurately traced: one Herr Erich Ostwald, now presumed dead. There were few details of the man himself, except to say that he was born into a prominent Berlin family and educated at the University of Strasbourg. He had been excused from war service after his older brother, Johann, had been killed in the battle of Passchendaele, and then, years later, had established himself as a successful member of the National Socialist German Workers' Party under Gruppenführer Graf von Hessen as part of the Berlin SA. From late 1931, his whereabouts were largely unknown. His death, likely accidental, book-ended a short and in some ways archetypal modern German life: Ostwald was a patriot and had died a tragic, wasteful death. Some of the article focused on the motorcar itself – an Adler saloon – with questions raised over the culpability of the Frankfurt manufacturers. Had the engine overheated? Had the petrol tank ruptured for some reason? Who was to blame?

This emphasis pleased Erich. The *Angriff* made no mention of his betrayal of the Party – there was no way they'd publicly admit to having a traitor in their ranks. If there was a bounty on his head, then only a select few would know about it.

Erich buzzed with relief. He looked outside where it was snowing lightly now and along the shabby boulevard

91

the shop fronts caught the powdery snow in their outstretched awnings. But as he stood at the window and began to unbutton his shirt, something outside caught his eye. Or rather someone caught his eye. It was the red-headed girl from moments before stood on the opposite side of the street looking up at the hotel.

Erich stepped back from the window and lit a cigarette. Something didn't feel right. He stood close up to the wall and glimpsed out of the window at an oblique angle. The woman was still there. A winter wind passed down the avenue and stirred up her coattails. The snow wheeled in circles as the breeze picked up, and Erich could feel the chill trickle through the gaps in his window frame.

Her face was very familiar – but who the hell was she? If he recognised her, then there was the possibility that he'd met her before. It meant he could take no chances. He thought back to his time as the double-agent working on behalf of the government. It was a basic rule of espionage that if you suspected something, you'd make damn sure you investigated it and stopped any threat in its tracks.

Memories returned. When he was operational in the ranks of the Nazi Party, his primary task had been to convince those around him of his dedication to the rise of the Party. Trussed up in a black tie, boots and cylindrical cap, the success of his cover depended on persuading others of this commitment. And then, when the make-believe began to crumble around him, self-preservation meant it was time to leave and seek out a more anonymous existence.

Was she one of them? He had to do something to find out and made his way to the lobby. He looked around the corner and waited for one of the bellboys to pass, one of the new ones who had just started their shift. Erich clicked his fingers to attract the lad's attention and waved him over. The boy – a pimple-faced teenager with blond hair – idled across the floor.

Erich spoke to him beneath the arches of the staircase. 'There's a telephone box across the road. I want you to get the number for that phone box for me. Here's a coin. Be quick about it.'

The boy nodded, took the coin and disappeared through the lobby. Erich remained where he was, keeping an eye on the entrance to the hotel. From where he stood he could see through to the street and to the telephone box outside.

Presently the errand boy returned. In his fingers he held a torn strip of paper. Erich gave the boy another coin and then went to the telephone booth on the far side of the hotel lobby. He dialled the number and after connecting, it rang.

'Answer,' he whispered to himself. 'Answer it.'

After about twelve rings the phone rang out. He tried the number again and let it ring for as long as possible. This time someone answered. Erich took three steps back and looked out into the street. He could see the red-haired woman had stepped into the phone box and was clutching the receiver in her hand.

'Yes?'

'Who are you?' Erich asked.

'Oh, don't concern yourself with that. I'm more interested in you.'

Erich remained silent.

'I just need a few thousand marks that's all. I'm sure a wealthy and well-connected man like you can help.'

'You've got me mixed up with somebody else.'

'No, I don't think so Herr Ostwald,' she said laughing.

Erich put the phone down. He looked outside and

found the telephone box was now empty. He ran out into the street and looked in both directions but she was gone. He went back to the hotel and raced up the staircase to his room. In the last two years he'd had his fair share of looking over his shoulder. To work for the *Abwehr* and then discover your cover had been broken is enough to send a shockwave even through the toughest agent. Whoever she was, he had to act fast.

It was dusk and the hotel reception was empty. Erich deposited a pile of banknotes on the desk and left. He went to the nearby canal, waited for a coal barge to pass, then dropped his stash of old clothes into the water. Laden with old bricks, the parcel sunk with a gurgle of bubbles.

Soon enough he would leave Berlin, away to Dresden or perhaps further afield. After a few days had passed he would begin setting up a new identity. New papers, identity card, birth certificate. He would write out a new personal history – a new town for him to grow up in, a new family, a school, new friends with a history of their own. He would memorise it completely. And if things went in his favour then in a year from now he could be living a normal life. He may even be able to see his son again.

But first, the issue of the mallet head had to be dealt with. There was no choice but to retrieve it, assuming it hadn't been found yet. There was no time to recruit someone else to do it for him so he would have to go himself.

Thirty minutes later, he was moving along the southern outskirts of the city. He took an empty tram to the industrial quarter and walked the remaining three miles on foot. He crossed several fields that were heavily bogged with mud. Poplars and silver birch trees stood tall and naked on the fringes of farmland, and the smell of allotment bonfires clogged the air like dirty incense.

It was getting dark as he trekked back to the site. A small ridge in the landscape rose up with a line of trees cutting across it. He found a path that took him to the top of the ridge; from there he could make out the black form of the destroyed motorcar in the distance. He kept to the confines of the woods where the floor was strewn with the soft mulch of decomposing leaves.

Tiny birds flitted between the spindly branches of holly and hawthorn bushes as he crunched through the woodland. He wondered to himself how these fragile creatures could possibly survive the cruel conditions of a Berlin winter, in such a cold and barren landscape.

Still, there was a type of freedom here too. Wide open spaces and not a single human in sight. It had about it the stranded quality of an impenetrable wasteland, as if nobody else could possibly have wandered through before him. Life out here would be cruel but affirming, if only survival were possible.

The impression of solitude was abruptly broken when he noticed a man walking across the landscape ahead of him. He was coming from the car, approaching along the track in the middle distance. He waved the beam of a torchlight in front of him. Erich crouched behind a bramble bush and watched. Was he the police? There would be little reason for a passerby to be on this track. He was wearing a wide-brimmed hat and a long overcoat. To Erich, he had the arrogant bearing of someone employed by the state.

For fifteen minutes the figure stalked the country spot, looping around in circles, before finally returning to the burnt-out car and away along the track.

Erich waited for as long as he could in the freezing conditions. Sure that the man had gone, he started searching the territory in decreasing circles. It was almost nightfall. He found the marshy pond and reached his arm into the icy water. Feeling around for the solid object, he wondered how deep the water was, so he snapped off a long branch from a nearby lime tree and plunged it into the water. The pond was about five feet deep, with small rocks and gravel at the bottom. He sifted through the water, covering the entire area. There was no sign of the mallet head block.

Then, all at once, an incredible chorus of cawing swept over into the treetops as a thousand black crows came in to roost. It was a thunderous wave that swelled in the sky and for a moment drowned out every last thought in his mind. Instinctively he dipped his head; at which, down on the ground, he saw something. It was a playing card. He picked it up and slipped it into his pocket.

He withdraw back into the woods and disappeared from view. That evening he slowly walked back to the outskirts of Berlin city. These were the silent edges, where mud tracks turned back into roads and the familiar sound of motorcar engines resumed. In his defeat Erich thought it would be in these middle territories, or more likely on the edge of some other city, that he would make his new base. Always in retreat, never quite settling, forever looking over his shoulder.

16

Arno Hiller left his office and went to get some dinner. On his way, he lit a cigarette and mulled over the latest news of the burnt-out car. It was already in the papers, so there would be additional pressure on him to supply some answers.

The discovery that the car belonged to Erich Ostwald had come as a shock. The man was an old accomplice; when Arno heard the name it conjured memories of a different time in his life, a time when Erich had been like a mentor to him. It was hard to believe he could be the same black ball of molten bones he'd examined at the motorcar window.

The last time they'd been in the same room as one another was two years ago when Arno himself had infiltrated the Nazi Party. It wasn't until Erich revealed himself as a special agent for the military police that Arno understood they were working more or less for the same side.

The thought that now occupied his mind was that if Erich was dead, then his betrayal of the Party could have something to do with it. Then his next thought followed on like a train carriage shunting into the engine, that he too could be a target of a revenge killing. Was he protected now he was part of Kripo? If the talk was to be believed, then the ascent of the Nazi Party into the ranks of government would mean sweeping changes for the police – and that meant nobody was safe.

Arno focused his mind on the task at hand. At the back of the restaurant was a telephone on a stand. He rang an old contact who would pass a message onto Lovis Blume.

'Get Blume for me. Tell him that Erich Ostwald is dead.'

He then changed his mind about the restaurant and left immediately.

At the same time, Thomas felt disillusioned. His oldest friend in Berlin had been burnt to death, and with the news his fortitude had been completely obliterated.

A thin covering of fresh snow had fallen across the city like a white veil. He walked for a while and eventually took himself to the plush quarters of *The Resi* on Blumenstrasse. He and Käthe went there sometimes in the week to meet up with friends. But tonight, he just needed a place to reflect.

The Resi was a dance hall and casino, famous for its water shows and live music. At the weekends, it was full of people who came from the suburbs to dance and be seen out in their finery. Sequins and black jackets, pearls and silk boleros. Foreigners were there too, Dutchman and English dignitaries, talking loudly and laughing about having too many parties to go to and not enough time.

The Resi was famous for other reasons too: as a place to meet potential lovers. It was all a game, but the enterprise was given an additional frisson of excitement by the latest technology: a series of pneumatic tubes that carried notes from one table to another.

The idea with the 'Pneumatic Mail Service' was simple. You wrote out an amorous message on a piece of paper, stuck it into a canister – like a message-in-a-bottle

– and then popped it into the snake-like tube attached to every table. Your message would get sucked up to the top gallery and a few moments later drop into the basket of your intended recipient. Many a love affair had sown its seeds using this method.

And love letters weren't the only item you could send. The establishment offered a veritable menu of gifts for visitors to order: bottles of perfume, cigar cutters, travel maps, all magically whisked around the room. And if you knew the correct codeword – so the rumour went – you could even order a bag of cocaine.

Tonight was a Monday and the dance hall was mostly empty. A few old dogs with wet cigars sat hunched over their drinks, whilst a piano player played an American jazz song in the corner. Thomas ordered himself a beer and took a schnapps chaser with it.

As he sipped on his drink, he let the news about his old friend sink through him. It was a sensation that seemed to have no definite beginning or end. Was Erich Ostwald really dead? Had it really come to this?

It had been five years since he'd last seen Erich. During the intervening years, time had built on top of itself like the steps of a staircase. He had never known where those steps were leading but he'd always assumed that they would one day take him back into Erich's company. But now, with this news, that idea had slipped beyond the realm of possibility.

Just then, quite out of the blue, he heard the pneumatic tube on his table come to life. It made a wheezing sound; seconds later a metal can dropped into his basket.

He glanced around. The dance hall had little more than twenty people in it. He thought he might see a woman flirtatiously gazing across the room at him. He took another sip of his drink and opened the canister, pulling out a rolled-up piece of paper.

'Mind if I join you?'

He looked up. A figure appeared before him and sat down in the chair opposite. It was Hölz.

'You sent this?' Thomas said, with a sneer of disappointment in his voice.

The newcomer smiled. 'I couldn't resist,' Hölz said, then resuming his more sombre look. 'I wanted to commiserate you on the news of your friend.'

'You have a funny way of commiserating,' Thomas replied.

'It seems as though there is a case to be investigated after all. Erich Ostwald is too interesting for this sort of thing to happen by chance.'

'What are you saying? It wasn't an accident?'

Hölz took off his hat and sat down.

'Anything is possible. I know about Erich's previous activities and it seems likely to me that he was intentionally targeted.'

The mention of Erich's history pricked Thomas' interest. What he knew about his old friend's dealings was thin on detail and was pieced together from other people's accounts, most of them from Arno. Despite years of friendship, Erich had always been elusive about who and what he was involved with.

'It's a complicated story,' Thomas said, doing his best to hide his ignorance.

'When a man has a foot in several camps at the same time, it can put him in danger. From what I understand, he had been walking a fine line for years. The agents of the *Abwehr* are never easy to track down, but it seems as if Erich was a little too eager to appear as the hero.'

'The *Abwehr*?'

'Military intelligence. Do you not know his background?'

100

'I was aware that Erich had been exposed as a spy.'

'Quite so. Two years ago he was revealed as an agent whilst operating undercover in the ranks of the Nazi Party.'

Thomas remained poker-faced.

'Actually, he was there to reveal duplicity in the ranks of the Prussian Police. Some officers were benefitting financially from passing information between the state and the more criminal elements of the Party.'

Hölz took out a pipe from his inside pocket and began to pack it with tobacco. He lit a match and started sucking on the end of the mouthpiece. Through an uncouth haze of smoke, he leaned forward to bring Thomas into his confidence.

'It must be a tremendous shock to you to hear about Erich's demise.'

Thomas sat back, pulling himself out of Hölz's smoky cloud. He thought back to when he'd suggested to Arno that the burnt-out car with a dead body inside could be politically motivated. After all, these days it wasn't unheard of for someone with a high profile to be bumped off in the middle of the night.

'What exactly are you doing here?' he asked, suddenly realising it was too much of a coincidence for Hölz to be in the same bar as him. 'Did you follow me here?'

'I'm here to help.'

'Shouldn't you be helping Arno?' Thomas replied. 'We don't know each other.'

'Fine. You've uncovered me. I'm here because I want to find out all that I can about Erich Ostwald. I'm ambitious. Will you oblige me?'

Thomas shook his head. 'You should be speaking Arno.'

'Arno is impulsive. He lacks professionalism.'

Thomas held up the pneumatic note again. 'Whereas you are a pillar of maturity?'

'Forgive me. That was just my way of breaking the ice.' Hölz leaned over to an artificial palm tree that stood nearby and tapped his pipe into the plant pot. 'Why don't we start again. I'd be more than happy to cooperate with your newspaper article if you are willing to help me in return.'

Thomas gave a little flick of his head to indicate his consent. After all, what did he owe to Arno anyway? His suspicions – that Arno found him wanting, and that Arno was more foolhardy and adventurous than he could ever be – were the only things he really felt sure of when it came to his errant brother-in-law.

'Why don't you tell me how long you have known Erich Ostwald?' Hölz began again.

'At least fifteen years. We met at an athletics club when we were younger. We began training together.'

As Thomas spoke, he began to remember the sight of Erich at the sports club, how every movement he made was awkward and perilous, how he sprinted with his arms and legs flailing like the limbs of a string-puppet, and how, due perhaps to his willingness to try anything once, he often managed to win whatever competition he entered. What a sight!

'Back then Erich was the sort of person who threw himself into everything,' Thomas went on. 'I remember, his favourite event was the high-jump. You've never seen anyone run and leap with such abandon.'

'What about a family. Did he ever marry?'

'He had a fiancée, Ingrid.'

'Children?'

'A son. As far as I'm aware, the boy has never met his father.'

'Why not?'

'Erich left for Spain five years ago – but then, you know all about that.'

'Of course,' Hölz replied.

Thomas fell silent. The spiral of tragedy he was beginning to foresee unravelling from Erich's death was woeful. The thought of Ingrid and her child finding out was like barbed wire to his being.

'Of course, there is another explanation,' Hölz said. 'That Erich Ostwald committed suicide. If Erich was on the run, he may have felt it was his only option, especially if his family might be in danger.'

'I don't think Erich would do that. He wouldn't give in like that.'

'You'd be surprised. I once knew a doctor who was on murder charges. Very sound of mind to speak to. He hung himself in his prison cell while awaiting trial. For some, it's a way of taking charge of fate.'

'Not Erich. That's not the man I knew.'

'Don't you see? He was a traitor. People wanted him dead. He'd operated as a Nazi official for two years and then betrayed them. Do you think they'd want a man like that out on the loose?'

Thomas didn't answer. It was time to leave.

Sensing this, Hölz got to his feet and took out a card with his contact details on. 'That's if you want to talk further.' He slipped his pipe into his jacket pocket. 'Next time we meet, I'll lend you my copy of the *I Ching*.'

It was late by the time Arno returned to his apartment. The light in the stairwell flickered as he climbed the steps to the third floor. The chilled stone felt so cold in the dead of night. When he got inside, he turned his stove up to full capacity and stood warming his hands in front of it still wearing his hat and coat.

He felt edgy and altogether solitary. The thought of

103

Erich dying in a car on that harsh stretch of farmland unnerved him.

He never felt like this in his old attic room, perhaps because it was so high up in the eaves of the roof that he felt invisible up there. In his new apartment it was different. He had a job and status; therefore he was no longer anonymous – and he didn't like the thought of it.

He went around and locked the door and windows. The silence of the apartment was interrupted only by the creaking of the stove. Would he be next? He simply couldn't ignore the question. Was he going to meet with the savage hands of a midnight assassin or was he exaggerating the threat?

And yet, if it could happen to Erich then it could happen to him too. They were not so different. They had both betrayed the Nazis. They both had scores that hadn't been settled…

Just at that moment, his thoughts were broken by the sound of tapping on his front door. He stopped and listened, then went and stood beside the entrance. It was late, nearly midnight. He deliberately numbed his mind to the question of who or what could possibly be behind it and braced himself as he reached for the latch.

He opened the door and found nobody there. Just an empty space, a vacant landing. He stepped forward and looked over the bannister, down into the vertical of descending staircases. There was silence.

Going back inside, he locked the door behind him. He returned to the stove, picking up a crust of bread to chew on as he warmed himself.

Then the tapping came again. He stopped chewing and listened. This time he recognised it as coming not from outside but from within his apartment. Someone was inside. *Goddammit.* The noise was like a fingernail tapping against the wall. Tap, tap, tap. He put down his crust of bread and moved quietly to a nearby chest of drawers. Inside the second drawer, nestled at the bottom, he kept a revolver. It was not officially assigned to him; instead it was an old military gun that he'd picked up from his retired uncle Konrad. Arno had never had cause to use it until now.

He took the revolver and moved cautiously through the apartment. The tapping stopped. He kept his eyes wide open. The light bulbs that hung from the ceiling were unshaded so the light they cast made deep shadows in all the corners. His suspicions were pulled in all directions, snagged by the merest creak of a floorboard, the slightest groan of a window in the wind. He turned to face one way then spun to face another. The gun in his hand was heavy, almost magnetic as if it was pulling him around like the arm on a compass.

Just then, all the lights in the apartment went out. The room fell into pitch darkness.

There and then, he felt tempted to pull the trigger, if only to send a shot crashing through the thickening silence. A bullet fired from the pistol would split open the darkness like a lightning strike. A flash, an explosion. It would destroy the darkness, if only for a moment.

'Come out, I know you're in here,' he said loudly.

Nothing. Then the tapping began again, this time followed by the sound of fingernails scraping against wood.

'Don't make me come and find you. I swear, I won't hesitate to shoot.'

Then he pulled the trigger. The room lit up in a flash. The bullet vanished into a wall. With the recoil, the revolver broke from his grip and fell to the floor. As it hit the ground it went off again, leaving it spinning on its barrel with the force of the shot.

Then a voice came from the dark. 'What the hell are

you doing?'

Arno grabbed the gun as the lights came on and saw the face of Lovis Blume step out from a cupboard.

'Why are you shooting into the wall?' Blume said.

'What the hell are you doing here?' Arno shouted at him.

'I've come with news.'

'You scared me to death! Why did you turn the lights off?'

'Your fuse box is in that cupboard.'

Arno rolled his eyes, what a wind-up!

'How did you get in here?'

'I took your key.' Blume held up a brass key.

'No, I have mine with me.'

'In the restaurant. I took it, made a pressing, then gave it back to you.'

'What?'

'When we were sat together. You ate pickled herring if I remember correctly.'

'That's sly. Pretty good.'

'I've got hundreds of keys. That's hundreds of opportunities if I need them.'

Arno sat down.

'I've been putting the word out about your case,' Blume explained.

'And what have you heard?'

'To cut a long story short, someone says they saw Erich Ostwald in the city on Monday night.'

'Monday? That was the day before the car was found.'

'One of the doormen at the Sing-Sing bar. He swears he saw Erich Ostwald there with another man. Says he knows Ostwald from way back.'

'Really? I'd better pay the Sing-Sing bar a visit then.'

17

The next evening Arno arrived at the Sing-Sing bar on Chausseestrasse and passed through the leather curtain that hung over the doorway. The room ahead of him was filling up. The atmosphere was sedate but had a certain ripening quality as if things could get very raucous later on.

He approached the counter and spoke to a waiter. He said he was looking for the doorman, the one who was there on the night of the Nazi procession, explaining that he had some business he'd like to discuss.

The waiter scratched his chin and thought for a moment before disappearing through the swinging doors of the kitchen. A few minutes later he came back with another man who announced himself as the manager.

'What may I do for you this evening?' the manager asked. He wore a red suit and a striped tie. A thin moustache ran along his top lip like a pencil line.

'The doorman who worked last Monday night? Is he here?' Arno inquired.

'May I ask why?' The manager pursed his lips. He had broad features with a jaw that stuck out ahead of the rest of his face, so that his mouth made a strange bowl shape. His head was shaved above his ears, whereas on the top of his head was a great explosion of wiry black curls.

'I want to give him a tip for his excellent service. I didn't have any cash on me at the time. I wanted to give it to him in person.'

The manager smiled with his odd little mouth. Arno noticed how his eyes constantly shifted left and right, always on the lookout.

'He doesn't usually work on Fridays,' the manager replied, 'but tonight, by chance, he happens to be coming in for an extra shift. That was lucky, wasn't it?'

Arno forced a grin.

'Have you been coming to Sing-Sing for long?'

'It's a real hotspot,' Arno replied. 'Nowhere else quite like it in Berlin.' He'd never stepped foot inside the Sing-Sing bar until tonight although he'd heard plenty of stories.

'I am delighted to hear it: a satisfied customer. I'm one of the few bar owners in this town who can proudly say that we've survived every storm the city can throw at us. The trick is to put on a show that is so outlandish that nobody can copy it.'

Arno noticed how the manager seemed to have grown by an inch as he spoke about his bar. As he went on, he began to make curious gestures with his fingers to express himself, as if he was threading an invisible thread into an invisible needle.

'Most people,' the manager continued, 'lack the imagination to come up with anything as preposterous as this. Ninety-nine out of a hundred people, if you ask them to open a restaurant, would do little more than fill it with chandeliers and marble tables and try to pretend we were in Paris or Vienna. That lack of ingenuity really does turn my stomach.'

'What time will the doorman be in?' Arno asked impatiently.

The manager checked his glistening silver wristwatch,

108

'In about twenty minutes. Please take a seat, you are welcome to wait if you like.' He led Arno to a bench in the far corner of the room, near to where a jazz band was just tuning up. A minute later he returned with a tall glass of yellow liquid and placed it down in front of Arno. 'Here, why don't you try one of our new cocktails. It's my own personal concoction.' He began to weave his invisible thread with his fingers again as a look of glee arrived on his face. 'I bet you can't drink it down in one go.'

'Is doesn't look like it's supposed to be drunk down in one go.'

'Why don't you try it and see? It has a peculiar quality, a thrill, if I do say so myself. Seems to me that the best things in life are enjoyed as intensely as possible.'

Arno picked up the glass and took a little sniff above the rim. It smelt like peppermint mixed with peach schnapps.

The manager sat down beside him and gave him a nudge of encouragement.

Arno put the glass to his lips. He could feel the vapours rising from the drink, realising it was a thick, gloopy substance like cough syrup.

'Go on. Give it a try.' The manager was wide-eyed with excitement. He sat there with shoulders hunched and his curious bowl-mouth trembling in mid-air.

Arno lifted the glass and let the yellow liquid slide into his mouth and down his throat. It was both cool and fiery, with a bite. The taste sent a jolt through him.

'Well?' The manager said, looking into Arno's empty glass. 'You did it! And in one go. How good was it? Was it *really* good?'

Arno was about to give an honest answer when an accordion player – dressed in the uniform of a prison inmate – sat on the bench beside him and began to gesticulate his instrument. Arno's response was drowned out by the playing, which for some bizarre reason the manager took as a positive response. He grinned wildly and patted Arno on the back before excusing himself with a flutter of his fingers.

Arno waited for another twenty minutes, jostled by the pendulum elbow of the accordion player. He was hungry, so he ordered Cervelat sausage with bread and butter and another yellow cocktail. It tasted just as unpleasant as the first time, but as the manager had said, it did provide a certain thrill in the drinking.

Finally, he got the signal that the doorman had arrived. He got to his feet and went towards the leather curtain. Waiting in an alcove was a tall man with a large head like a pumpkin. His hair was greased back in loose, oily strands. He carried a confident swagger, stood with his thumbs hooked inside his trouser braces, swaying from side to side to give the impression that he wasn't to be meddled with.

'I heard you were looking for me,' he said.

Arno noticed that one of his ears had an entire lobe missing. He reached into his pocket and pulled out a couple of notes which he screwed up and pushed into the doorman's palm. 'A little something for you and your hard work.'

The man took the money and deposited it into his breast pocket with two thick fingers.

'There's more of that if you can answer a couple of questions for me.'

The doorman lurched to one side, propping himself up against a wall. 'Go on.'

'I'm looking for information on a man named Erich Ostwald. I'm told that you saw him here on Monday.'

The doorman lit a cigarette and took his time to

answer. 'Who's asking?'

'You don't need to know that.'

'Then I can't help you.'

'So the word *Libelle* means nothing to you?'

'Oh, so you're Blume's man? In that case, let's take a seat.'

'You claim to have seen Ostwald last Monday?'

'Yes, that's right.'

'How do you know it was him?'

'He's been coming in here for years now, on and off. Don't get me wrong, I don't know him to speak to. We've not said more than three words to one another in all that time. Only, he stands out for being generous with his tips. Look around you, this isn't the sort of place where the upper-classes tend to frequent. He's unusual in that respect.'

'And I hear he was with someone that night? Do you know who?'

'Never seen him before in my life.'

'Could you describe him?'

'Short blond hair, clean-shaven, I'd say he was about mid-forties. He wore turn-ups on his trousers and workman's boots.'

'Did you notice anything else?'

'Well,' the doorman said pridefully, taking a long drag on his cigarette. 'I had my eye on them because Herr Ostwald nearly always comes here alone, so it was unusual to see him with anybody else. I noticed them especially because they seemed to be excited about something. They were talking into each other's ear, like they had a secret between them.'

'So they knew each other?'

'Couldn't say. But I did hear them exchange details about their backgrounds, so no, I wouldn't think they knew each other very well.'

'What else do you remember about this man?'

'Firstly, he had a bag of tools with him. In my line of work you have to look out for those sorts of things. Anyone coming in here with a bag like that – must have a watchful eye over them.'

'How do you know it was a bag of tools?'

'Because he left it open on the floor and I came by to have a look inside.'

'Did you see anything unusual?'

'No, only wrenches, spanners, a wooden spirit level.'

'Nothing at all?'

'Well, not until this gentleman took out a knife from his bag.'

Arno raised his eyebrows. 'A knife? And what did he do with it?'

'They were looking at it together, then he handed it over for Herr Ostwald to inspect. He removed the wooden sheath, which of course, really hooked my attention. They seem to be examining it with sheer admiration.' The doorman checked around him to be sure he wasn't being overheard. 'I would have gone straight over there had it not been Herr Ostwald. Someone like him, you learn to leave alone.' The doorman dropped his cigarette on the ground and crushed it beneath the toe of his large boot.

'And what happened next?'

'They chatted for a while. I think they ordered some food. The bar was getting busy at this point, especially with all the celebrations going on that night, so my attention became divided.'

'How long were they here for?'

'Oh, I don't know, about an hour, at a guess.'

'Any idea where they went to afterwards?'

'Haven't I told you enough?' The doorman stood up straight and adjusted the braces on his trousers.

Arno dug around in his pockets looking for some more cash. He pulled out a handful of loose coins and let them fall into the doorman's open palm.

'Is that all you got?' the doorman huffed.

'Listen,' Arno said. 'Do you know where I'm from?'

'I know that you've been in contact with Lovis Blume. Who you're working for is another matter.' The doorman said these words with an intentional sneer, making it clear he didn't care one way or another who Arno was.

Arno refrained from divulging that he worked for the police, knowing it was wiser to remain known only through his underground connections.

The doorman shifted his weight. 'Look,' he said, cracking his knuckles, 'I owed Blume a favour and now I've repaid that debt. This conversation is over.'

'Listen to me, you know what happens to people who don't stand by the code?' Arno stared the doorman in the eyes and quickly clicked his fingers. 'They get kicked out of the circle, they get shunted out and then they're anyone's game.'

'Why are you looking for Ostwald?'

'I believe that Erich Ostwald is dead and it's possible that the man you saw him with was his killer. I'm tracking his last movements.'

'You're tracking a murderer? I wouldn't have said a word to you if I knew that.'

'Look, it's important I find out who he is. Anything else you can tell me means you're protecting our network and working against our enemies.'

'I've told you all that I know.' The doorman wiped his greasy hair back over his head, saying, 'There was one other thing. It could be nothing.'

'What is it?'

'When they left – Herr Ostwald put his arm across

this man's shoulder and said, *Enjoy your stay.*'

'Enjoy your stay? Sounds like he wasn't from around here.'

'Could be.'

'Come on, think man.'

'They were talking about Berlin and they mentioned the Excelsior.'

The Excelsior Hotel was a majestic establishment on Askanischer Platz just across the street from Anhalter train station. Arno knew it well. It was in the district of Kreuzberg, not far from his old attic room. It was one of those grand-looking buildings that had more than a passing resemblance to a Roman temple.

'You're sure it was the Excelsior?'

'Positive.'

Arno shook hands with the doorman and passed him another banknote in the same gesture, one he'd been holding back as a final flourish. The doorman gave an ambiguous sort of grin – it was hard to say if he was grateful for the tip or underwhelmed by it.

As Arno left the bar, the manager with the wild hair approached and escorted him to the leather curtain.

'That cocktail still giving you a buzz?' he said suggestively.

'Not at all,' Arno replied. He had what he wanted; there was no need to play the game anymore.

18

Arno woke the following day and immediately sent word to Thomas to meet him at his apartment. Without backing from Kripo, he realised that Thomas' willingness to help out was becoming invaluable, especially now that Erich was in the picture.

The only thing was he had to keep Thomas' involvement somewhat invisible. Too many visits to the office on Alexanderplatz and people might start to question who this outsider was and what exactly he was doing in police headquarters. It was better to invite Thomas to his place where they could talk freely.

'Let's go through what we have so far,' Thomas said as he entered.

'I want to show you this.' Arno led the way to a large art deco style cupboard in the corner of his living room. It was made from walnut and looked about a hundred years old. He turned the little metal key and pulled back the door. Pinned to the inside was an array of newspaper clippings and hand-written observations, along with a map of central Berlin.

'This is everything we know so far,' Arno said as he pressed an image of an Alder saloon cut from a magazine to the cupboard door.

'What's the latest then?'

'Thanks to the doorman of Sing-Sing we now have a

suspect. We have a description of a man who was in close conversation with Erich. The doorman also said that this companion was carrying a bag of tools. Wrenches, spanners, a wooden spirit level, that sort of thing.'

'So he was a tradesman?'

'Perhaps. But it sounds like he was a stranger, not from these parts. *Enjoy your stay* – they were the last words Erich said to him as they left.'

'So he was visiting? Maybe a tourist? But why would he be carrying a bag of tools if he was in the city on holiday?'

'That's what I've been wondering too.'

'And?'

'What if he was in Berlin to fulfil an assignment? After all, by the end of the night, Erich was dead.'

'And the bag of tools? Surely you don't think he was carrying his weapons with him in plain sight?'

'Why not? A killer disguises himself as a tradesman. He's just going about his business. A man like that blends in.'

Arno crossed the room and went to warm himself by the stove. He opened the hatch and sifted through the hot cinders with the small shovel, bringing them back to life with a crackle. His gaze drifted towards the window. In his mind he saw the knife: as yet he hadn't mentioned his recovery of it from the car wreck to anyone. It was possible he'd made the most important discovery so far. But his instincts told him to keep it to himself. Besides, the case was in his charge and it was up to him to lead it as he saw fit.

'Did you mention a wooden spirit level in the tool bag?' Thomas asked.

'That's right. Why?'

'It makes me think of the wooden block you pulled

out of the pond. I wonder what it is.'

'Why? Do you think it could be another tool?'

'If it was a tool, then it was broken at the circular point on one side, which suggests the missing part was also round or maybe cylindrical in one dimension.'

Both men paused in thought.

'A handle perhaps.'

'If you imagine the shape of the wooden block and a round handle together, then you would have a hammer. Could it be the head of a mallet?' Arno said with his eyes widened.

Thomas looked over. 'A mallet from his tool bag.' He let loose a smile, then immediately checked himself as an image of Erich Ostwald being bludgeoned to death with the blunt instrument sprang to his mind.

'The doorman at the Sing-Sing bar made no mention of a mallet inside the tool bag.'

'It could still belong to him.'

'I will get it examined,' Arno said eventually, giving the coals a forceful prod and sending up a rush of dancing sparks.

'For fingerprints?' Thomas asked hopefully.

'For whatever we can find. We have microscopes now – and they can see a hundred times more than the naked eye.'

Thomas nodded.

'There's another thing. During their conversation, the doorman heard mention of the Excelsior Hotel.'

'Oh?'

'It seems odd that he would choose the Excelsior. Why not stay somewhere cheaper, somewhere less ostentatious?'

'No, it doesn't stack up.'

'My thoughts are we should visit as soon as possible.'

'Today?'

'I need to go to the office first, but I'll meet you at the hotel in an hour.'

Arno arrived in his office and was soon joined by an officer from the forensics department. He explained that the wooden block needed some tests and handed the bagged item over. It was at this point that Hölz stepped in through the door. He was wearing his wide-brimmed felt hat, which he made a great performance of taking off, brushing it down with his fingertips and hanging it on a coat peg with care. Arno glanced over at the new arrival with a scowl.

'If I may interrupt? I couldn't help but overhear. Are you sure that the item in question was not already contaminated?' Hölz took his seat on the opposite side of the desk.

'It's really nothing to do with you,' Arno replied.

Hölz unravelled the black scarf that was looped around his neck and stared at Arno. 'When I attended college, we were instructed in detail about the integrity of potential evidence. We were told that contamination is a constant threat to our investigation. That was one of the wonderful things about our training, that we were fully instructed on these types of things. But then, I don't suppose you believe yourself to have missed out, do you my friend?'

Arno felt his fist clenching but then relaxed.

'Didn't they teach you about soot-powder and adhesive tape?' Hölz went on.

'I don't recall, did they?'

'For collecting fingerprints? It's very basic.'

Arno had never received the tuition that Hölz was talking about, but he got the gist. He thought back to the remote dirt track with the car on it and how he had handled the mallet head. If there was useful evidence on

118

that implement they could be tarnished now. He felt foolish in front of Hölz but didn't show it.

'I always follow the correct procedures,' he said. 'Be in no doubt about that, *my friend.*'

Hölz lifted his briefcase onto the desk and delved into its jaws. 'If you wish to deliver a murderer to justice, you must have solid evidence to present.' He pulled out a pack of playing cards and set them to one side. 'I'd make that your priority if I were you.'

Arno had heard enough. He left the building and went to reconvene with Thomas.

They came in from Askanischer Platz and entered the lobby of the Excelsior Hotel. It was one of the grandest hotels in the whole country, maybe even the entire continent. Conveniently placed across the street from one of the main train stations of Berlin, its six-hundred rooms and nine restaurants catered for an international guest list. There was even an underground tunnel connecting the hotel to the station across the road.

The building stood with stained glass windows and large rugs spread over the wooden herringbone floor. In the centre of the lobby was a great bronze statue of a nude woman, Victory or some other sleek goddess from ancient Greece.

It was the middle of the afternoon and the hotel carried a sedate atmosphere. A few tables were taken by afternoon coffee drinkers who chatted and clinked their cups into saucers. Luggage boys stood around looking bored, waiting for their day to heat up with new arrivals and new opportunities for a cash tip.

Arno approached the reception. When nobody noticed him waiting, he announced himself loudly and solemnly. 'Detective Hiller.'

Eventually, a receptionist came over at a leisurely

pace. He was perfectly turned out in a black waistcoat and glowing brass buttons. 'May I help you sir?'

'My name is Detective Hiller. I'd like to see your guest book.'

'I can't do that sir. We offer our guests the utmost discretion.'

'It is a police matter, so I expect your cooperation.'

The receptionist looked bewildered.

'Maybe you could answer a couple of questions for me? There may have been a man staying here, three or fours nights ago. He was a tradesman. You may have seen him carrying a tool bag. Ring any bells?'

'Do you have a name, sir?'

'No, but we do know he was roughly mid-forties, had short blond hair and was clean-shaven.'

'A tradesman you say?'

'Yes, staying as a guest.'

'You mean he was working here and staying here?'

Arno started to get ruffled. 'We're talking about someone who has potentially committed a serious crime, so concentrate on what I'm saying.'

'That seems very irregular. You're going to tell me he was a pianist next!'

Arno was just about to lunge at the receptionist when Thomas tugged him back.

'Just think back to several days ago, around the time of the chancellor's procession,' Thomas appealed. 'Did a tradesman come here, not to work but to check in as a guest? Someone who wouldn't usually stay here?'

The receptionist thought for a second. 'No,' he said.

'Thomas, this is going nowhere.'

Meanwhile, a woman emerged from behind a satin curtain.

'Leave this with me,' she said, before dismissing the first receptionist, who scurried off, muttering and flapping. The new attendant then proceeded to take out a large gold watch from her waistcoat pocket and compared it with the electric clock on the wall. 'You say you're from the police?'

Arno nodded.

'I finish my shift in ten minutes. I'll speak to you when I clock-off.'

Arno and Thomas sat down in two dark-wood armchairs. Fifteen minutes later, the receptionist appeared in a flared flannel skirt and a heavy pullover. She led the visitors up the marble steps of the formal staircase. They went into a small annexe room on the first floor. It was cold and dimly lit. In the corner was an old stove. They sat down on chairs with threadbare cushions, hardly the same level of decor as the rest of the hotel.

'What can you tell us?' Arno asked.

'That man with the tool bag?' she responded. 'You don't forget a man like him in a hurry.'

19

The receptionist had blonde hair plastered back against her head. Whatever she used to hold it in place, it seemed to have solidified into thick, brittle ridges. She had pale freckled skin and a beauty spot pencilled onto her cheek.

'I'm quite certain I know who you're talking about,' the hotel woman announced. She seemed oddly excited to speak – or impatient to vent something on her mind.

'What do you remember about him?' Arno asked.

'That odious man? It's among the virtues of a good receptionist to notice everything and everyone. That lobby out there – it's a turnstile for the entire world. Besides which, he was unforgettable. Uncouth is not the word. From the countryside, of course. You could cut his crassness with a knife. We don't normally get folk like him in this hotel. The cost of our rooms – if you will – tend to filter out the undesirables. But this particular one seemed to have slipped through the net. He claimed his stay was a gift to himself. Or so he told me.'

'He lacked discretion then?'

'He told everyone. What was it he said? *It was the greatest day in history!* What a barbarian.'

'Day?'

'He was here for the procession you see, to watch Hitler get sworn into office. The greatest thing to happen to this country since the birth of Bismarck, were his words if I remember correctly. Bought himself a fancy hotel room to enjoy the occasion.'

'So he was a Nazi supporter?'

'Oh yes. One of those who maintains a certain pitch of enthusiasm for their cause. He'd even volunteered his time to help put up all those disgusting flags you see swinging from the sides of buildings.'

Thomas took out his notepad and began scribbling. 'That would explain why he had the tool bag,' he said as he wrote.

'Do you keep addresses of your guests?' Arno asked.

'Neuruppin.'

'Neuruppin?'

'That's where he was from. Neuruppin. The thing you have to remember is that we don't usually have folk such as him staying here. Our owner, the esteemed Herr Elschner, once had to remove Hitler himself from the hotel on account of other guests threatening to leave if he was allowed to stay. The Nazi Party have since boycotted the hotel, which – I have to say – is not such a terrible outcome.'

'So as a Nazi advocate, he stood out?' Arno confirmed.

'That's why I remember him so clearly. You might have thought he had a stake in the place, the way he strolled in and out with his bag of tools slung proudly over his shoulder.'

'A social pariah then?' Arno put to the receptionist.

'As I say, you have to keep your eyes peeled. There's more to this job than most people give us credit for.' The receptionist rubbed her hands together as the chill of the room began to bite.

'There's one more thing we need from you,' Arno said. 'A name. We need the man's name. And his full address.'

'Is that so?' The receptionist suddenly fell mute and crossed her arms. 'Is he in trouble?' she asked, pretending she hadn't heard all their previous conversation from behind the reception curtain.

'He might be. He might very dangerous. That's why you have to help us. A name. Please.'

'I can do better than that – for the right price.'

'Better?'

'He hasn't checked out yet. The man's still here.'

'He's still at the hotel?'

'His room is still occupied.'

'My god,' Thomas said with a stern look.

'We ask all our guests to inform the front desk of their departure in a timely fashion to avoid being billed for a further night. As yet, that man is still being charged for his room. I haven't seen him this morning, so as far as I know, he could be upstairs right now.'

Arno looked at Thomas. Both men got to their feet and began for the door. 'Which room?' Arno demanded.

'Room 417,' the receptionist said, grinning. 'For 100 marks, I can let you inside.' At this, she went into her pocket and pulled out a key. 'I came prepared,' she said.

Arno looked at Thomas again – who was already digging in his jacket pocket and pulling out a bundle of banknotes.

'Here are 50 marks for coming forward, take it or leave it,' Arno said bluntly.

The receptionist snatched the money. Along with the key, she handed over a slip of paper. When Arno unfolded it, he read out the name of their suspect: 'Wolfgang Mayer.'

20

Outside the room, the corridor was empty, with just the sound of water trickling through the central heating pipework that ran overhead. They moved quietly but at speed. Room 417 was midway along the passageway on the fourth floor. When they reached it they found the door had one of those *Please do not disturb* notices hanging from the handle. It showed a porter's face with his finger 'shushing' at his lips.

There was no telling if Mayer was inside or not. Arno thought he might have brought his revolver with him. He began to check his pockets for some other object he could use as a weapon if the occasion required.

He put his ear to the door and listened for signs of life. There was no sound. He took the key given to him by the receptionist and gently slipped it into the lock. When he turned it, the key jammed and the lock seized.

'Damn.'

'What's happened?' Thomas whispered.

The key was stuck in a quarter-turned position. He tried to move it again without making too much noise. The last thing he wanted was to give the man inside forewarning of their arrival.

'Just keep a lookout,' Arno said, glancing up at Thomas.

He turned the key in the opposite direction and

removed it completely from the door. Kneeling down, he put his eye to the keyhole. He thought the occupant may have blocked the barrel with something, but there was nothing to be seen.

At that moment, an elderly couple both with white hair and a sheen of wealth, came out of an adjacent facing room. As the husband locked their door, the wife took a moment to inspect the two men loitering in the corridor opposite.

'Good afternoon,' Thomas said politely as he smiled.

'Good day,' the woman responded.

'Actually,' Thomas said, engaging the couple. 'Can you tell me? Have you noticed anyone come or go from this room today?'

'I'm sorry?' the woman said, widening her eyes to suggest she hadn't caught the question.

Arno got up off his knees and pretended to brush himself down. 'We're from hotel maintenance, here to fix this door.'

The elderly couple smiled vaguely as if they hadn't understood a word spoken to them. 'Come on dear, it's time for afternoon cake,' the husband said. He took his wife's arm and together they shuffled away.

'What are you doing?' Arno flared at Thomas.

'They might have seen Mayer.'

'We have to be more discreet.'

Arno returned his attention to the door. 'I'm going to knock.' Before Thomas could respond, Arno was rapping his finger-knuckles against the door. There was no response. 'Room service,' he announced and knocked again.

When no answer came, he put the key back in the lock and put all of his weight behind it, swiftly squeezing it in a full circle. At last, the door opened and they went inside. Arno first, Thomas second.

'Be careful,' Arno said, taking charge.

He stepped forward and looked around the room. The bed was unmade. And on one side of the room there was a desk with several empty bottles of Riesling. A pair of suede shoes lay kicked off in a corner. The curtain drapes were closed and the smell of stale cigarettes rose from an ashtray full of butts.

The two men entered and began to scout the room. As he closed the door behind him, Thomas said, 'He's not here now but it looks like he's spent the night here.'

'I wouldn't expect him to be here. Only a fool would stay in the city after what he did.'

'You think he's fled?'

'Why would he stay? At least we have a chance to collect evidence. But first, take some photographs, a snapshot of this room would be extremely useful.'

Thomas took out his camera and proceeded to move around the room, capturing its state.

Arno then took one of the pillows from the bed and pulled the stuffing from inside. He put on his leather gloves and used the empty pillowcase as a bag to collect up items. He found a used comb and put that inside, and with it an empty wine bottle and one of the suede shoes.

Thomas called over. He was standing beside a water jug and basin that was overlooked by a pair of silver taps. 'There are some nail clippings in here.'

'Gather them up and we'll bring them with us.'

'So you think he's left the city by now?' Thomas started up again. Being in the hotel room, among the possessions of the man they were pursuing, gave him a chilling sensation.

'Just think about it. Would you hang around? My guess is that whoever was in this room left on the night of the 30th. Or if not then, the day after.'

'What I don't understand,' Thomas replied, 'is why

he would draw such attention to himself here in the hotel? The receptionist said he was loud and uncouth. You'd think he'd be the very opposite and do his best to stay invisible. Instead, he made a great show of himself as if he *wanted* to be noticed. That doesn't make sense to me.'

'Wait,' Arno said noticing something under the bed. As he carefully drew it out, he knew he'd hit his target. 'I think this proves we're in the right place.'

Thomas looked over. 'The tool bag!' he proclaimed.

Arno used his foot to dislodge the mouth of the bag so the two sides fell open. Inside was just what he expected to find: a wrench, several pliers, a pinion hand drill, a gouge chisel and the wooden spirit level. He bent over and began sifting through the metal objects. It was all dirty inside the bag, with a residue of grease and sawdust coating everything.

Just then, the door to the room clicked.

Arno stood up and put his finger to his lips as he grabbed Thomas and pulled their backs against a wall. Together they watched as the door handle turned and began to open. Arno shifted his gaze to a mirror hung on the wall. In it he could see the door from a different angle: whoever was about to come through it, he would catch them in the mirror. He glanced at the tool bag at his feet. Was there enough time to bend down and grab the wrench?

Then he realised that he too would be visible in the mirror. He tried to step out from the reflection, but it was too late. The figure had seen him and was already turning on their heels.

'Stop,' Arno called. He scrambled past the bed and went in pursuit. Thomas followed as they bundled through the door together. The figure was already halfway down the corridor and moving at a decent pace.

They followed on in a dash, their smooth-soled shoes sliding on the carpeted floor.

'Mayer,' Arno shouted after the running man.

The figure ahead careered around a corner and ran down the stairs in a flurry. They went after him with unblinking speed. By the time they reached the top of the marble staircase, the man was already a floor below. With Arno in front, they trickled down the stairs at a pace, their feet tapping over the steps, circling with the curve of the staircase as they moved from floor to floor. Soon enough they were bumping through the crowded lobby and through the revolving doors.

Out into the great square, amid the criss-cross of motorcars and tram-lines, they could see the figure dashing towards the train station opposite.

The Anhalter Bahnhof was a huge looming edifice built out of steel, stone and glass. The sound of locomotive whistles echoed from behind the great walls. Before the station, the steady circus of travellers and market stalls spread out beneath the naked branches of winter trees. Arno and Thomas crossed the road and passed over a patch of frosted lawn. Motorcars lined up at a junction, waiting for the double-carriage of a passing tram to slide by.

They dodged the tram. Then a man carrying a suitcase stepped out from nowhere and crashed head-on with Thomas, but he quickly got to his feet and picked up the pace. Soon they were beneath the archway of the station entrance and racing into the hall. Red swastika flags left over from the celebrations hung from the girders of the roof. Snaking plumes of steam wound upwards from the trains and pressed against the banners in a ghostly dance.

Ahead of them, their man was skipping left and right between passengers on the crowded platform. He

129

jumped over a row of empty luggage trolleys and ran at full tilt along the platform towards a train that was just pulling out. Remarkably, he managed to grab hold of the final carriage and hoist himself aboard. He slipped in through the rear-most door as the train picked up speed and carved its way out of the station.

Arno and Thomas came to a stop on the smoky platform and could do nothing but watch the locomotive disappear around a bend.

'Damn, we missed him,' Arno said between heavy breaths. Thomas didn't respond. He'd not run like that in years and his chest was feeling the bite.

Arno approached the nearest station guard. 'Where's that train going?'

'All the way to Hamburg,' the guard replied.

'Does it stop on the way?'

'Fifteen times all told.'

'Can you get it stopped?'

The guard shook his head. Arno looked down the empty track, then glanced at Thomas.

The two men walked back along the platform, their thoughts crowded out by the din of the station and a sense of sheer disappointment. A steam whistle blew and a great column of soot rose up like a charcoal cypress tree. They made their way back to the hotel using the purpose-built underpass that returned them to the lobby of the Excelsior.

They quickly went back to room 417 to retrieve the evidence inside. Arno also wanted to collect the tool bag before searching the room for a final time.

'I can't believe we nearly had him,' Thomas said still buzzing.

'We'll get him next time,' Arno said sifting through every cupboard and drawer he could find. He recovered nothing else of significance. Then as he opened the last bedside drawer, he picked up something unexpected; a cheque for 4,000 marks written out to Wolfgang Mayer, signed by no other than Count Hermann Graf von Hessen.

'Hessen,' Arno said astounded.

'Who is he?

Arno had previously been forced to acquaint himself with the Nazi Gruppenführer, a high-ranking official who represented everything he detested about the Nazis. His association had cost him immensely.

'He's bad news. Come on, we'd better go, we're done here.'

Arno put the cheque with the other collected items. Between the fingerprints on a wine bottle and the nail clippings from the washbasin, there had to be grounds to identify Mayer. They had Mayer's tool bag and had also discovered what seemed to be a payment. But for what? What exactly did Mayer have to do for such a sum?

As they left the hotel and crossed the square, Arno turned to Thomas and said, 'We might need to get ourselves to Neuruppin. But first, we need to get these items investigated.'

21

Erich spent the night in a boarding house, where the damp walls and cracked windows kept the icy night at bay. After some haggling, he managed to get a room to himself where he could hide away until morning. His surroundings were barely visible in the candlelight where he lay deep in thought before sleep finally took him away.

He left the premises at dawn, feeling chilled to the bone but ready to get on with things. More than anything, he was desperate to leave Berlin and start afresh, but his problems were multiplying.

Not only was there the dilemma of the mallet, but he now also faced a new issue – the redhead in the beret. She knew more about him than he could tolerate. She knew he was alive, and that fact had to change. Who the hell was she? He felt sure she wasn't part of the police investigation; even so, she had somehow worked out that he was supposed to be dead. And she intended to use that knowledge to bribe him.

He traipsed through the city suburbs. The sky above was misted with winter rain. He found a café to have breakfast in and watched the yellowish pall sweep through the street on the other side of the rain speckled window.

What he needed was to find the redhead again. He

remembered that she'd first appeared outside the Excelsior Hotel. He bumped into her just after he'd planted the cheque in Mayer's room. Was she connected to the hotel? Perhaps she'd seen him come and go and had followed him through the city? Whoever she was, she'd seen through his disguise.

There was only one thing for it. He'd have to go back to the hotel. If that damned woman was there, then she might come out of the woodwork. He had to take the risk.

He made his way to the Excelsior but was conscious of his dishevelled state. It would be all too easy to draw the wrong sort of attention to himself, to be mistaken for a vagabond or worse risk being recognised from his previous visits.

And so he decided a new image was required. His cash was beginning to run low – soon he'd have to make a visit to the bank and access the account he'd set up under an alias – but for now he still had enough in his pocket to buy a new suit and get a shave.

Three streets away from the hotel, along a damp alley where cats roamed, he found a gentleman's clothing shop that catered for the more unusual and ornate end of men's fashion. They sold razor-thin neckties, silk vests and had a rack of leather long-coats. Inside was also a barbershop advertising the 'Essential men's haircut: the *Herrenschnitt*.' It was perfect, Erich thought as he stepped in through the door. An hour later, he left the damp alley looking like a new man, dressed in a fine suit complete with a trilby.

As he ambled towards the Excelsior, he kept his eyes peeled for the woman. He slipped into the hotel as a guest, discreetly touring the lobby and checking each of the restaurants in turn. He spent some time moving

133

through the various reception rooms of the hotel, yet the red-headed woman was nowhere to be seen.

Without any sign of her, his attention soon turned to room 417. Mayer's room. He wondered if the police had made the connection yet. Had the trail from the Sing-Sing bar back to the Excelsior and Mayer's hotel room been picked up?

If only he could just take a look. Unable to resist, he began moving up the marble staircase, quickly finding himself on the fourth floor. When he reached room 417, he waited for a moment. There was no security on the door or the suggestion of a police cordon. He listened and thought he could hear movement coming from inside the room. Maybe it was the hotel staff inside? After five minutes, when nobody had emerged, he gently pushed on the handle and slowly eased back the door a couple of inches. His view into the room was aided by a mirror hung on the wall. In the mirror, he could see the outlines of two men.

They weren't wearing the hotel livery, and when they fell silent he knew they'd become aware of his presence. Without waiting to find out more, he turned and briskly walked away.

He heard them call after him and felt their pounding feet following along the corridor. He began to run as his long legs took him down the grand staircase at a pace. He attempted to retain some decorum as he crossed the lobby but realised they would soon be on his heels. There was no time to consider if he might be recognised now. Drawing attention to himself was impossible to avoid.

He slid through the revolving doors and raced between the passing buses across the road. A woman with a fish stand, who stood wrapping headless fish in newspapers, shouted at him to slow down. He ignored her and ran on, slicing through the crowds of people. A very large man with a bowler hat and a blond moustache took two steps aside to let Erich pass. Soon enough he was inside the station. There was no time to buy a ticket. He was aboard the first train he reached. It didn't matter where it was going to. The train burrowed through its own cloud of steam as it eased away.

He glanced back through the train carriage window and saw the panting form of the two men who had been in pursuit of him. They were bent over with their hands on their knees. Thank god he'd got away. Then it was only when they raised their heads that he was instantly gobsmacked. For he knew them.

Arno Hiller. And behind him, Thomas Strack. He recognised them instantly.

It seemed inconceivable. What were they doing here? Was it really them chasing him? Arno Hiller and Thomas Strack?

He found a compartment to sit in and nestled himself in the corner, turning up the collar on his coat to shield his face. Looking out of the window, he thought about his old companions. He knew from a newspaper he'd read some time ago that Arno had joined the criminal police. The article described the expansion of the agency and Arno's name was mentioned in a list of new recruits. Had Arno been assigned to the case? Erich deliberated to himself as the train cut its way through the city suburbs and sped north. Perhaps Arno had forced his way onto the investigation. Had he heard about the burnt-out car, found out who it was registered to and then insisted he take over? It was possible.

And Thomas? What was his purpose?

Whatever the reasons, Erich suddenly began to see his situation in a different light. Was it possible he could make use of his old companions and somehow re-

135

engineer the situation he found himself in?

For the last five years of his life, he'd become estranged from his former attachments. His friendships had ceased along the way, not least with Thomas, and it was by no means obvious what reception he'd receive from them if they encountered each other again. But still, this discovery had changed things.

With all these thoughts, he felt neither fear, nor regret, nor shame or hope. All he felt was the suggestion of a new set of actions ahead of him.

He sat and watched the Brandenburg countryside pass by through the train window, as farmland appeared and disappeared between green embankments and pockets of forest. Was this to be his final farewell, or was it the beginning of a different course?

PART IV

22

Käthe and Thomas' city apartment was a combination of both old and new. The building itself could be dated back a hundred and fifty years, but the interior belonged strictly to the 1930s. The furniture was made of tubular chrome and Danish teak, and included a pair of art deco armchairs – from the design studio of no less than Jindřich Halabala. It was a splendid apartment, both overtly stylish and subtly restrained at the same time.

To live in the heart of Berlin was one of Käthe's longstanding dreams. They had resided there since their wedding day four years earlier. It had taken some getting used to for Käthe. The city was a liberal hotbed of wild nightlife and pleasure-seeking. It was bright and heady with creative experimentation and art all around, as well as music and cinema. But there was also something dark about the place, an undercurrent of poverty, criminal activity and prostitution, even on your own doorstep.

Late one evening at a quarter-to-midnight, two weeks after they'd moved in, Käthe saw a pair of women on the street below. One of them had feathers in her hair that caught the light from the streetlamps. The other held an ice-white scarf that she repeatedly drew around her neck and then removed, almost as if performing a signal. They were huddled into a doorway in the building opposite, staying close to one another, peering down the street.

Then a man approached. At first, Käthe only saw him by the orange ember of his cigarette. As he came into the light, she could see the cigarette was perched on his lips beneath the rim of a bowler hat. He was a spindly man, tall and narrow, and the hat he was wearing shielded the top of his face. He stood uneasily, a little fidgety, moving in and out of the shadows like an eclipsed moon. His long coat was buttoned up to the neck and for a moment Käthe assumed he was discreetly soliciting the girls for pleasure.

But watching on she realised the transaction was passing the other way: the girls began searching through their clutch purses and counting out a palm-full of coins. They tipped the coins into the man's cupped hands; in return he reached into his coat pocket and handed them something. Whatever he was handing out, he gave one to each girl, both of whom slipped their new possession into their cleavages.

Then there was a discussion. Or more of a disagreement. The girls began to raise their voices; Käthe could hear the woman's shrill protestations through the window glass. In return, the man made a vile sort of hissing noise that caused the women to become aggressive. Then, by way of response and with alarming swiftness, one of the women kicked him in the thigh whilst the other took out a knife from beneath her skirt and thrust it forward. She plunged it into the man's top shoulder, with venom. And as soon as her friend had reclaimed the money they had just given him, the knife was withdrawn and they dashed across the road.

As they disappeared between the passing coaches and away into the night, the bowler-hatted man fell forward, clutching his shoulder. Käthe was about to go out to help him, until she saw him pull himself up and lurch away in the opposite direction.

She found that night she couldn't sleep. She began to wonder what life was like for those two women on the street and what it was that had brought them to the point of carrying a knife they were so very willing to use.

That incident prompted something inside her. She felt she could no longer persist in her middle-class lifestyle with its glitzy society gatherings and expensive luncheons. Realising she had a desire to change things, it wasn't long before she took a deeper interest in women's rights. She joined the Berlin branch of the League of German Women's Associations and gave donations in support of their journal *Die Frau*.

She learned that many women fell into dire straits out of desperation. They simply didn't fit into the template that the politicians expected and turned to prostitution and drugs to get by.

For the girls who took the 'correct' path, many married young, rarely later than twenty-three and often several years earlier. The first task of a young newlywed was to conceive a child. Beyond that, she had to serve her husband, support him in his career and maintain the bonds that tie a family together, bearing and nursing babies, and tending to their husbands. That was the German way.

At the same time, a new generation of women had grown up, furnished with education and endowed with wider horizons. Käthe was one such woman, and she knew the contradictions that women like her faced. To obey the expectations of society was to embrace the many conflicts of women's rights and lack of choices.

When the organisation became split over the issue of women's reproductive rights, Käthe was firmly on the side of emancipation. A woman's body was her own, she argued, as was her right to contraception. 'Sex without intent to procreate is *not* a sin' was one slogan she got firmly behind.

In the early stages of her learning in these matters, Käthe became particularly inspired by a Jewish teacher by the name of Bertha Jacobs. Jacobs had helped set up a rescue home for unmarried mothers and illegitimate children in the centre of Berlin. 'We call it *Mutterschutz*,' Jacobs explained. 'The protection of mothers. And for the children, *Kinderschutz*. We try to give these girls a future by training them for jobs they might like to take up.'

Yet with the rise of the Nazis, a new type of pressure was emerging. Already the group had received notice that to continue they would have to submit to supervision from the Party. Käthe was incensed. But time was running out. Any Jewish members had to be listed and notice sent to the Party. Bertha Jacobs was among the names submitted.

'They hate movements like ours,' Jacobs told her on their last meeting, 'because they think we're encouraging women to abandon their roles. A man serves his country by fighting in battle. A woman serves by bearing strong children. As far as the Nazis are concerned, any woman who wants to live her life freely is a threat to the natural order of things. But I say, if the birth rate is falling, don't blame women who are educated and self-sufficient, blame the men who repressed us for so many centuries.'

Käthe began to predict worse was to come. She heard rumours of a policy for forced sterilisation for anyone who didn't fit the German mould, from Jews to gypsies. 'They talk of improving the stock, from generation to generation,' she told Thomas. 'It's disgusting.'

By the end of January that year, Bertha Jacobs had left the country after several threats to her life and the

League of German Women's Associations had begun to wind down their activities.

Käthe continued to volunteer at the rescue home, which remained open after Jacobs' departure. The girls she worked with were irrepressibly earnest in helping the needy. For them, the chance to contribute also meant a chance to aim an arrow at their own freedom. To their credit, this basic truth was not lost on them: to take action meant that at least some portion of their lives belonged firmly to them, despite the ever-changing whirlpool that was Berlin…

The night before, Thomas had come home to Käthe in a state. At first, he couldn't say what had happened but she coaxed it out of him. He told her that a car with the dead body of his oldest friend inside had been found. The whole thing had been set alight and all that was left was charred remains. The police had just traced the car and it belonged to Erich Ostwald.

'My God, what happened?'

'Nobody knows. An accident. Maybe something more sinister. We're not sure.'

A sense of shock filtered through Käthe. But then she knew Berlin could be a violent city.

'Arno's been assigned to the case. I must do what I can to help.'

'Erich was involved in all sorts of surreptitious things. Is it safe for you – or Arno for that matter?'

'I really couldn't say,' Thomas said, shaking his head. He wandered off to pour himself a drink, leaving the conversation only half complete. He lifted the stopper out of the glass decanter and trickled a brandy into a tumbler. As she watched him she could see he was completely devastated.

'Come Thomas, pour me one will you.'

Together they sat up into the early hours talking and remembering times they had shared with Erich. Thomas and Erich had been firm friends once. And despite their disassociation in recent years, Erich's death was still cause for lament.

The next day, Käthe had to go out. She'd received a telegram from her friend Jana Constein the painter, requesting that she visit her urgently. So she wrapped up in a thick scarf and coat and made her way across the city. It was one of those winter mornings when rays of sun streamed into every window, tree canopy and shop front. The sky was a steel sheet of pale blue and the air was crystalline in its iciness. She passed three nuns in their habits taking a stroll and a man in a wide-brimmed hat who bid her good day.

When Käthe arrived at Jana's, her studio was empty. But the door was open, so Käthe went in to wait. The narrow windows glinted with sunlight. Across the room, rows of canvases stood stacked against a wall. She tilted a picture towards her so she could see the front. It showed a girl looking into a compact mirror. Women appeared often in Jana's work: female tennis players, a girl alone in a bar, a nude in front of a mirror. Her subjects were entirely modern, each figure she painted bold and inquisitive.

Käthe went to the window to see if she could see Jana coming down the street. Instead, she saw a café with people drinking from small china cups at simple wooden tables. Next to it, she watched a shopkeeper sweeping the pavement at the front of his jeweller's shop. The shopkeeper was a tall, stooping man. Through his grey trousers, you could see he was very thin, all bone and tight ligament. He had a long face, pointed like a trowel.

She wondered where Jana was. Then on hearing a noise behind her, she turned expecting to see the artist enter. But it was not the artist who stood before her. It was Erich Ostwald.

23

An hour earlier, Erich had taken himself into a telephone box and pulled the metal door shut. He lit a cigarette and sucked on it repeatedly to coax the tip into life. The phone box filled with grey smoke that lolled over the iced glass like mist on a cold lake.

He had sent Käthe a message, saying it was imperative that she travel to Wilmersdorf to visit her friend Jana Constein as soon as she could. If he went ahead with this gamble, there would be no going back. The outcome of such a step was unpredictable but it could also advance his position. Nonetheless, a very distinct part of him remained ambivalent.

The telephone box was hidden around the corner from the apartment. Across the street was a gambling parlour with a sign that read, 'Don't let luck pass you by.'

Just then, a man with a briefcase began tapping loudly on the telephone box door. 'Are you going to be long?' he barked in a shrill voice. Erich pretended not to notice. The man could see the telephone wasn't in use and tapped again, this time using his wedding ring against the glass. Erich was about to send the man packing when suddenly he saw Käthe emerge from the apartment building. She was dressed in a long winter coat and a blue scarf wrapped around her shoulders.

He barged past the man and began to follow her. She

got onto a tram; he slipped onto the same carriage at the rear and kept himself hidden. When she got off at Wilmersdorf and walked to the studio of Jana Constein, he continued to trail her from behind. It was a district he knew well, but he hadn't expected to be back there again.

Remaining set back, he climbed the steps after her. Käthe's back was turned when he entered the studio. She was looking out of one of the windows. Erich stared at her. He pictured himself grabbing her from behind, cupping her mouth to silence her before revealing himself.

But he thought better of it and instead moved a chair so that it made a scraping sound, upon which Käthe turned. Her smile was already in place, ready to greet her artist friend, ready to say something complimentary and warm, but when she saw Erich her smile crumbled away like dry pastry.

'Hello Käthe,' he said after a moment of silence.

She looked at him with a deeply vexed expression.

'It's Erich.'

She remained mute. It was Erich who stood before her, true and immediate. The very man who, less than twenty-four hours earlier, she'd been told was dead. But here he was. How was it possible? And then the thought: what did he want?

'What are you doing here?'

'It seems odd, I know. A lot has happened since we last saw each other.' He went to step towards her but she flinched back. 'I expect you've heard the news by now, about the car that was found and the body inside. But people must believe I am dead now. I know it seems strange and I'm sure you have lots of questions, but for now, I simply want you to listen to me.'

Käthe felt apprehensive but consented with a vague nod.

'The burnt-out car did indeed belong to me. The man inside was someone I met and befriended. But he turned out to be a nasty piece of work and we got into a fight.' Erich then paused. 'What can I say? He was going to stab me. What could I do?'

'What did you do?'

'I defended myself.'

'My God,' she said, taking an involuntary intake of breath. 'Is he the body in the car?'

Erich nodded. 'It was my only choice. If I'm going to live the rest of my life without constantly looking over my shoulder then I had to do something like this.'

'That doesn't sound like self-defence.'

'Perhaps it doesn't,' Erich confessed. 'Look, I have my reasons. You're a friend, I know that I can trust you. I can trust you, can't I Käthe?'

'We're not friends,' she said. 'You tried to deceive Thomas with your scheming and then you left. And now you're telling me you've killed someone? You're deluded to think I'll help you!'

She went to make a dash for the door but Erich blocked her path.

'I wouldn't do that if I were you.'

Käthe looked at him. Her next question was simple and direct: 'I'm assuming you sent a false telegram to lure me here. Where's Jana?'

'I sent her an anonymous note to get her out of the way.'

'So you tricked her too.'

'Look, I need your help.'

'I can't help you. Nor can Thomas.'

'The weapon that I used to kill him has been found. A wooden mallet. I intended to throw it onto the bonfire but in the haste of the moment I was unable to. Now I need you to help me.'

148

'How am I supposed to do that?' Her voice brayed with disbelief.

'Thomas is involved with the investigation is he not – I've seen him and Arno together? It's true, isn't it? Thomas and Arno are working together, aren't they?'

'Thomas is writing for a newspaper. And Arno is acting as the lead detective.'

'Writing for a newspaper? That's good. Yes, that's very good.' Erich went on. 'That means Thomas can be an influence.'

'You've taken leave of your senses.'

'I want you to pass a message on to him. I can't speak to Thomas directly. It's too risky. You mustn't even tell him that you've seen me today. At least, not when you're inside your apartment.'

'Why? What's wrong with our apartment?'

'Nothing that I know of. But you never know who could be listening. Besides which' – Erich paused deliberating whether to continue or not – 'your brother might be in danger.'

'Arno? Why?'

'Because he also has a troubled history with the Party. It's been two years now but the people who monitor these things have a long memory. I can't say anything for certain but we should expect the worst. You should talk to Thomas with caution.'

She nodded. A strange convulsion passed through her.

'Did you have to kill someone?'

Erich lowered his head in admission. Then, lifting his eyes, he said, 'When there are no choices left, the unthinkable suddenly becomes an option. I've been on the run for two years now and the Nazis won't stop until they get their hands on me. I have a price on my head and all they want is vengeance.'

149

'Why?'

'Because I conspired against them.'

Käthe was confused. 'Don't the people who recruited you offer some form of protection?'

'Now the Nazi's have entered government, there is no real protection for me.'

'And what of Arno? Is he…' Käthe stopped as the interruption of footsteps sounded outside the studio door. Erich hid behind it as the door swung open, through which Jana entered.

'Käthe, my dear,' she said surprised.

Käthe went over and kissed her on each cheek. 'I wanted to surprise you, I have news from Bertha Jacobs, she's written to me.'

'Excellent. I've just come back from a prank call. But thank God it was a false alarm. Shall we make ourselves a drink?'

'I could do with one right now,' Käthe said as she went into the other room with Jana. As Jana began chatting, Käthe looked back into the studio. The room was empty – Erich was gone.

24

Thomas sat in his apartment and worked on his article for the *Frankfurter Zeitung*. Käthe had gone out for the day to visit her artist friend Jana Constein. Whilst she was out, he would take the opportunity to distil all his notes down into a first draft. He had to remove any particulars connected with the case and arrive at a concise *impression* of the gritty side of Berlin – the city where he'd lived for over a decade.

The commission from the newspaper was a breakthrough. It had taken nearly thirty 'pitches' to various newspaper editors to get his foot in the door. There were the left-wing papers such as the *Berliner Morgenpost* and the Social Democratic Party's *Vorwärts*. And there were right-wing papers too, with *Der Angriff* being just about the most extreme of them.

He chose to focus most of his efforts on the *Frankfurter Zeitung*, which was just about the most influential liberal newspaper in Germany. It also had its famous *feuilleton*, an idea they'd borrowed from the French: a supplement to the main paper set aside for literature and criticism, fashion and epigrams. The *feuilleton* would be the perfect place for Thomas' sketches to find a home.

The *Frankfurter* took a long time to bite. The only two pieces they deigned to sniff at were about the luxurious hotels of Berlin and a piece about the seedier side of Berlin's nightlife.

The second of these gave him the idea to write about the criminal aspect of the city – and as soon as he'd thought of it, he knew Arno would be indispensable. He pitched the piece as a feature to the *Frankfurter* and the newspaper liked it. The editor responded with enthusiasm, suggesting – remarkably – that Thomas could turn it into a series. When all the negotiations were done, it was agreed that he would write six 1,000-word sketches that would build to present the facets of the city's underworld.

And then it came to the actual writing. He'd thought to begin with a memory of his own arrival in Berlin, beginning in 1921. He would recall them as 'wild years.' It was a time when people abandoned themselves to pleasure. The war was still a recent memory and you had the feeling that everyone needed to go deranged for a while in order to repair themselves.

Bars opened at a frantic pace. Prostitution was never so rife. If you wanted to, you could buy guns and ammunition practically anywhere. A steady trickle of Mauser rifles – the same model 98 used by the army – returned to the city and began appearing on market stalls and in the windows of shops that didn't care to hide them.

Music changed. Gone were the Viennese waltzes in the traditional ballrooms; in their place American jazz, banjo strings and the woozy sound of saxophones wafting from cellar doorways. Cinemas started opening. Comedians in cabarets teased everyone about the raucous side of Berlin. War casualties sat twisted on every street corner, some of them real, others undoubtedly fake. Then inflation began to rise and a strange resignation took hold, almost as if everyone knew it was coming – like a kind of inevitable plague. The mark began to tumble against foreign currencies, slow at first but every day getting faster.

Circumstances like these were bound to go one of two ways: either they would end up in a utopia or a hell. And with humans being the way they were, it looked like the answer had arrived. That said, it was still a shock to see a man being beaten up before your eyes or a troop of SA men standing in front of a Jewish shop demonising its existence. These things remained notable for their hostility, as if they didn't quite fit into the rhythm of the city. They were not typical to begin with, more like random misfortunes. It was only when you thought about it more deeply that you began to connect the dots, that a darker force was looming.

At the more benign end, you could hardly go a day without having a collection tin or pamphlet shaken in front of your face, usually belonging to a Stormtrooper promoting their rightful cause. They often came into cafés and restaurants, and even if the proprietors didn't want them hassling their customers, they were usually too wary to refuse them entry. Which was worse? A few customers made to feel uncomfortable or a broken nose and a brick through the window? It was easier just to let the men do what they wanted.

The more brutal end of the campaigning occurred out on the street. Of course there were the posters with grand statements and promises that were as vacuous as they were attention-grabbing: *We want work and bread. We want Hitler! One people. One leader. One vote. Fight with us for peace and equality. Vote for the Leader!*

With the Nazis on the verge of power after Hitler's appointment, the Stormtroopers could be unleashed with impunity. That's what the Stormtroopers wanted all along: a green light to take their fight out into the open.

153

Hitler's chancellorship had somehow made it seem legal, as if the SA were now the rightful force of justice of the country. And so they spent the month of February harassing and intimidating people – all under the banner of 'Law and order.'

It wasn't just the Communist left they had in their sights. The SA men even began attacking right-wing parties if they saw them as too conservative. The Nazis harassed and beat up men from the steel helmet brigade, *Der Stahlhelm*, mostly made up of the old veterans from the war. It seemed like nobody was safe.

As Thomas wrote, he began to think of his own life and most of all, of his life with Käthe. He remembered how excited she was to come and live in Berlin. She had glowed with anticipation as they explored the bars and restaurants and cinemas together. But when the stock markets crashed then the changes came, and the sense that Berlin was the centre of the high-life gradually faded. That was when the fascists began to win the arguments instead of being dismissed as extremists.

Thomas' mind then turned to the memory of Erich Ostwald, who all through these changes had been absent from the city and yet somehow always present. Perhaps it felt that way because he was the sort of man who would turn up at any moment, whom you may not have seen for weeks at a time but who would, all of a sudden, turn up at your door, most likely bearing a bottle of elbling and a glistening grin of disobedience.

He pictured his old friend. The tall frame. The dark-auburn hair. The sharp features of his face. Always dressed in expensive tailoring and always ready to indulge. He liked to tell stories and be among a crowd. Especially if that meant making people feel uncomfortable with his horseplay.

He remembered once when Erich took him to a

154

party at a grand residence in Wilmersdorf. Thomas had never known anything like it. Champagne, caviar on blinis, almost as many waiters as guests. And how did Erich behave among the higher echelons of Berlin's beau-monde? With sheer contempt! He pretended to be drunk, he pinched the backside of a diplomat's wife, he flung his arms around an old man in a top-hat and a monocle, raising a toast to 'Alexander the Great – who should have been a German!'

It was sheer nonsense, all of it. That was the Erich that Thomas remembered the most, the man who enjoyed nothing more than to flirt with decadence, using a combination of charm and prankster's wit. The man who took delight in seeing the shocked faces of the black-tie-and-tuxedo crowd, with the bubbles in their glasses trembling in private panic. Erich Ostwald was a cross between a talented good-for-nothing and socialite genius.

He would seldom talk about serious things, like personal responsibility or anything that didn't involve a form of pleasure. There was no one else quite like Erich…

Thomas brought his focus back to his writing. He made a plate of spätzle and continued to type into the evening. Then, at about eight o'clock, the telephone rang. He thought it might be Käthe. She should be home by now. He answered. The line was silent for a moment, then a voice spoke. On the other end was Bernard Hölz.

25

Hölz was waiting on a bench when Thomas came outside. He was wearing the same wide-brimmed hat as he always did; beneath its overhang a tobacco pipe let off a drift of smoke. He rose up, coming towards Thomas with an extended hand, and theatrically blew a gust of fog into the nighttime air. Thomas winced inside – he could see that Hölz was trying too hard.

'I know it's late,' Hölz said. 'But I wanted to talk to you alone. I know that Arno can be a touch unconventional – I feel sure you understand what I mean.'

'You said you had something important to tell me. It's late and it's freezing. I should be at home with my wife right now.'

'But your wife isn't at home.'

'Who says?'

'A hunch. You wouldn't have come out if she was. Don't you find that marriages can get in the way of being free to do what you want? I prefer to remain single for that reason. Or perhaps you are not as independent as I am.'

Thomas looked Hölz up and down.

'Have you come here to insult me?' Thomas asked.

'Never,' Hölz went on, 'I can see to have a wife as pretty as yours, then marriage must be more appealing.'

'How do you know what my wife looks like?'

'Surely you're not denying that Frau Strack is an attractive woman?'

'You're wasting my time,' Thomas said as he turned to leave.

'Wait. I do have something that I wanted to pass on. I think it could be useful, both in the investigation and in your writing. Perhaps we should find somewhere warmer where we can talk?'

Thomas thought of his typewriter back at the apartment. The article was spinning off in all sorts of directions. Maybe a short break with Hölz would revive his focus.

They walked together in silence towards a flashing neon light where Thomas knew a late night café would still be serving.

'What have you got to tell me?' he asked, as they took their seats in the empty hall of the café.

'Well, that all depends on how you are getting on in your search for the killer.'

'You should ask Arno if you want any details.'

'That is precisely what I cannot do,' Hölz said. 'Arno is full of bitterness towards me. There was a reason we were assigned to the same office. Or did you not realise that?'

'What?'

'That one of my duties is to keep an eye on him. Think of me as a mentor. I am quietly nudging my student in the right direction. I have been through all the correct recruitment stages. Senior detective trainees must have gained their *Abitur* before they are even considered for the selection process. Personally, I came from the lower ranks of the police, which is the preferred route. I'm here to help Arno grow – the trick is to allow him to think he is making all the decisions.'

'But you take the reigns when the moment suits you?'

'All I really want to do is help. We all want Arno to be a success.'

Thomas peered over Hölz's shoulder, wondering where his coffee was. The lone waitress behind the counter seemed more interested in tuning her radio than preparing his order. The later the hour got, the more impatient he grew.

'What is it you want to know?'

'Come, don't be on the defensive. Arno and I are part of the same organisation after all.'

Thomas raised his hand and tried to signal to the waitress. It didn't make sense to him why Hölz, who was professionally schooled, would come to him.

Hölz went on: 'There is another consideration. Arno's background is not as clear cut as some in the police would prefer. Perhaps you might think about the implications of that for a moment?'

'How do you mean?' Thomas said, his attention caught by Hölz' change in tone.

'Simply that Arno's allegiances must remain under suspicion. He has, after all, had his fingers in various pies during the past several years. My understanding is that you yourself were a victim of his duplicity some years ago. I don't wish to drag that up. My point is a simple one, that where Arno is concerned, none of us can ever be quite sure that he's as transparent as he presents himself. It is for precisely that reason that he must be steered in the right direction' – Hölz held up his palm as if he was making an oath – 'It could make all the difference to his future. I'm merely asking for your assistance in this very important concern.'

Thomas watched as Hölz slowly laid his hand down onto the tabletop. There he left it, with an expression frozen on his face that said he was quietly satisfied with

158

his little speech.

Thomas considered for a moment. What Hölz said was certainly true. Arno did have a shady history and Thomas suspected he knew only a fraction of it. He wouldn't mention this to Hölz, but he had long thought that Arno was too erratic for his own good. There was a part of Thomas that admired these qualities and at times wished he had some of that unruliness himself. But now, being sat with Hölz, whose pressed trousers and starched shirt spoke of a certain self-respect and authority, he knew that there was also something powerful in taking the *correct* approach to life. Perhaps he and Hölz were not so different. They were both conscientious and sure-footed. More importantly, sharing what he knew with someone from officialdom may help Erich's case further.

'Very well,' Thomas replied.

Hölz displayed a smile. 'Good.'

'We were told that Erich had been spotted at the Sing-Sing bar. He was there with another fellow.'

'Who told you this?'

'It was a tip-off from one of Arno's connections. Don't ask me how he knows this individual. Apparently, the doorman of the Sing-Sing had seen Erich with his companion during the evening and was able to supply a reasonable description.'

'This contact of Arno's, I'd like to know more about them.'

'There's not much more I can say. I've never met the man.'

'What about a name? Does this individual have an identity?'

'His name – let me see – is Blume. Lovis Blume. He and Arno go back many years, so far as I know.'

'Is he trustworthy?' Hölz asked.

'Well, Arno holds his opinion in high regard so I

159

have no reason to doubt him. At the very least, he was able to locate Erich on the night of his disappearance. If it wasn't for Blume, we would never have got our testimony from the doorman.'

'I see,' said Hölz. 'So this Blume fellow has connections across the city? And he was able to use those connections to pinpoint Erich Ostwald to the Sing-Sing bar? And you're confident that Arno has been completely truthful about this?'

Thomas disregarded the question. He was still waiting for his order to arrive. He looked at his watch – it was nine o'clock. The waitress was still playing with the dials on the radio. He knocked on the table three times with his knuckles to grab her attention. This seemed to do the trick; she came over with two mugs of coffee and a cake on a small plate.

'Why don't you tell me about the doorman at the Sing-Sing bar?' Hölz said next.

'I can only report what Arno told me.'

'You didn't speak to the doorman yourself?'

'No. Arno went alone.'

'So you cannot verify the testimony?'

'Do I need to? Arno told me that the doorman had seen Erich and another man together, apparently looking like old friends and sharing jokes between them. This other man had a tool bag with him. It was from the doorman that we were able to gather that the suspect has been staying at the Excelsior Hotel.'

'And what makes you think that he is a suspect and not just an innocent companion?'

'He is the last person we know of to have seen Erich alive. Within hours of their meeting, Erich Ostwald was dead.'

'And did you visit the hotel?'

'Yes, but something tells me that you know that

160

already.'

Hölz gave a little smile of consent. He had one of those smiles that pulled his face to one side, as if only half the muscles of his face worked. 'Oh, I don't know anything about this. Do continue.'

'On the surface, he was in Berlin to watch the parade and celebrate the new chancellor.'

'On the surface?'

'We assume it was a cover for his real purpose.'

'To kill Erich Ostwald?'

'That's right.'

'Do you have proof for that conjecture?'

'No. But we managed to gain access to his room. I think we confirmed it was the same individual seen in the Sing-Sing bar. There was a tool bag. Undoubtedly it was the same man.'

Thomas was about to describe the events that followed, about the chase through the train station and then discovering the cheque on their return, but he held back from being so liberal with his information. He had said enough. Was he compromising Arno's investigation? Then again, if Hölz's experience could help with the case, then maybe it could help Arno too.

'And did anything come from the connections made in the hotel room?' Hölz asked.

'We are certain that we interrupted the suspect. He returned to the room whilst we were inside and fled as soon as he saw us. Unfortunately he got away.'

Hölz took a tiny sip of his coffee, almost as if to drink nothing at all, and then nodded. 'Well, this *is* fascinating. You have a body and you have a suspect. You know where he has been staying and I expect you know where he comes from too.'

'I fear we have scared him off,' Thomas added. 'Where he is right now is anyone's guess.'

'I wouldn't worry about that too much,' Hölz said.

'Why not?'

'I just wouldn't. Things will work out for you.'

Hölz stood up from the table, leaving his coffee hardly touched. He turned and then strode out of the café without saying another word.

26

Following the chase from Mayer's room, Arno returned to Askanischer Platz. He bought a newspaper and pretended to read it. Later, he stood beneath a sycamore tree and let a shoe-shiner polish his boots. All the time, he kept watch on the Excelsior Hotel and the Anhalter train station.

So far, he'd seen nothing suspicious.

He considered how doubtful it was that Mayer would return to the hotel. Perhaps he was already crossing a border into another country. The question was, why did he return in the first place?

Arno could take a trip to the town of Neuruppin. They had Mayer's address, or at least the address he'd presented to the hotel. The chances of it being his real address were slim, of course. But if everything in Berlin dried up, then Neuruppin would be the obvious next step.

As he kept a watchful eye he noticed there were three men from the *Sicherheitspolizei* loitering at the hotel entrance. They were called the 'Green Police' on account of their olive uniforms: they were security police, paramilitary in the main, sent out to subdue riots and any other public disturbance that might be deemed a threat to law and order. Arno often saw them hauling ropes up and knotting them around tree trunks and between lampposts in preparation for another march, ready to coerce the crowds one way or another. The majority of their ranks were made up from the *Freikorps* and officers from the old German Imperial Army. And most of all, these men were used to aiming their rifles at someone they didn't like the look of.

The men who stood outside the hotel were heavily armed, questioning people and watching them enter and leave through the revolving doors. Arno wondered what they were doing there, but made the assumption it was to do with the elections. The numbers of Green Police had been growing every day since the federal elections had been called for March time and electioneering had begun in earnest. Germany would see a great push by the National Socialists to win overall power, and this naturally meant a much greater chance of fights and riots breaking out.

Arno wished he could remain detached from the details. But it was hard to ignore the propaganda machines and the canvasing steadily proliferating across the city. Whatever tactics of persuasion the Nazis or the Communists wanted to employ, no one was immune to their slogans.

He continued to watch the hotel. When the Green Police moved on, he took himself back into the Excelsior. This time, he didn't visit the reception. He passed directly through the lobby, rounded the bronze sculpture of Victory and took a right-turn through to a restaurant. There, even before being shown to a seat, he ordered lamb chops and potatoes frites. From a discreet table, he watched the comings and goings. When his food came, he ate it slowly and maintained his surveillance.

By now, the restaurant was beginning to fill up with early evening diners whose soft chatter created a humming atmosphere. When six o'clock came, he slipped out from the restaurant against the traffic of residents coming down for dinner. He made his way up the marble staircase. Checking behind him, he went into the staff quarters where the receptionist had led them before. Six o'clock was mid-shift. There should be nobody passing through at this time.

Once inside the staffroom, he went to the far wall. On it was a display, a montage of items he'd noticed before, and within it something that had been niggling him since.

There were several objects that celebrated the hotel's history: a certificate of excellence from the Berlin Tourist Board; a silver rosette etched with the names of staff members recognised for their dedication. And at the centre of this wall of honour, there was a photograph.

He inspected the image. Framed in silver, it showed a gathering of faces lined up in a row, an array of men in suits staring honourably out of the frame. The man at the very centre of the image, around whom everyone else was assembled, was Curt Elschner, the owner of the Excelsior.

Arno was aware of Curt Elschner through the Berlin press. He owned a series of hotels across Germany, each one being bigger and more successful than the last. In Hamburg, he put the Hotel Esplanade on the map. And in 1919 he took over the Excelsior in Berlin and had turned it into the palace that stood today.

Yet it was not the face of Curt Elschner that Arno was interested in. Beside him in the photo was another man. He wasn't someone Arno recognised, not directly anyway, but still his eye was drawn to him. It was uncanny, but the man who stood beside Curt Elschner had a remarkable likeness to Erich Ostwald.

Undoubtedly it was *not* Erich. The man in the

165

photograph was at least ten years older, maybe double that. But in the blur and grain of the picture, if you merely glimpsed at it, you could certainly be forgiven for thinking that it was indeed Erich Ostwald who appeared there, his chin held up high and the slight tremor of a smile on his lips. Since it wasn't Erich – Arno concluded – then it could be somebody very close to him. A relative, an uncle, or maybe even his father. In short, Erich's family was linked to this hotel, he felt sure of it.

It was at this moment that Arno realised he needed to find out more about Erich Ostwald's background. There were the obvious details: the wealthy family, its links with industry and trade, Erich's expensive education and his privileged ability to step in and out of well-paid positions. But where exactly that privilege hailed from was unknown.

27

Walking along the tree-lined paths of the Tiergarten, Käthe and Thomas held hands and kept an eye out for the lively sparrows and blackbirds that flitted between the branches. Thomas was telling his wife about a time when he and Erich had taken a trip together in the winter to hike around Wannsee Lake but Käthe seemed preoccupied.

She gripped his hand and led him through a group of evergreen trees, beneath the stretching boughs of a Lebanon Cedar, where the long pine-laden branches created a secluded space hidden from the rest of the park. Thomas had the excited sense that his wife had prearranged this detour and was intending to proposition him in some way. He kept his eyes peeled and watched her as she let go of his hand and went to sit on one of the lower branches that doubled as a bench. He sat beside her and readied himself for some sort of illicit pleasure – whatever she might have in mind.

'I have something to tell you,' she said. 'It's important.'

'What is it Käthe?'

'I can't pretend it won't come as a shock.' By the tone of her voice, it was obvious that her intention was not to seduce him in this shadowy corner of the Tiergarten. In fact, her eyes were downcast and she looked a little pale.

Thomas could see it was something serious. 'You haven't met somebody else have you?'

'Of course not!' she said clutching his arm. 'Why would I want someone else!'

'Then what is it?'

'I've seen Erich Ostwald.'

'What?'

'I've seen Erich. He followed me to Jana's studio and he spoke to me.'

'What are you saying?'

'Thomas, listen to me. Erich Ostwald is alive. That's why I brought you here to the park, to tell you.'

Thomas looked at her quizzically.

'Erich said I mustn't speak to you about him whilst we're inside our apartment, in case someone is listening in. So I brought you here instead.'

'But the body in the car... his car... we are supposed to be hunting for his killer.'

Käthe took a deep breath and in one unbroken report explained what Erich had told her. She remembered what he'd said word for word in order to remain objective in her disclosure.

Thomas listened without interruption. When she had finished, he rose to his feet and gazed up at the sky. He had only one question to ask.

'And Erich confessed to killing a man?'

'That's what he told me, yes.'

'In order to fake his own death?'

'It's hard to believe isn't it? He must have been desperate.'

'Why did he come to you? Why not to me or Arno?'

'I don't know.'

The couple fell into silence. Nearby, out of sight, the sound of children playing came trickling through the tree branches. Eventually, Käthe spoke up again. 'There's another thing. He wants us to help him.'

A wry smile spread across Thomas' face. 'Is this another one of his tricks? Another hoax that he's willing to drag you into?'

'I don't think it's like that.'

Thomas shook his head in disbelief. 'No, he's got himself into a serious mess, now he has to deal with the consequences.'

'But…'

'Käthe, don't you see. He'll just use us.' Thomas began to pace. 'If we help him, we'll be incriminating ourselves in everything he's done. Whatever that is exactly.'

'Thomas, I know how you feel. But isn't there a part of you that is relieved, that he's alive?'

Thomas shut his eyes for a moment. 'Yes, of course I'm relieved.'

Käthe got up and scouted around the sheltered trees to make sure no one was within earshot. 'Listen to me,' she whispered as she signalled for him to come closer. 'He mentioned a wooden mallet. Erich said that it was the weapon he used.' She stopped herself. 'My God this is terrible, that we're talking about this.'

'What did he say about the mallet?' Thomas insisted.

'He said he used it to kill the other man but left it at the scene unintentionally.'

Thomas then paused. 'We found the head of a mallet, Arno and I.'

Her eyes widened in alarm as Thomas looked at his wife.

'He's worried that the mallet will incriminate him. He wants us to get it back for him.'

'That's not possible. The police have it. It's with the homicide office now. It's in the case notes and will be counted as evidence.'

'We must do something,' Käthe said.

'Why? You already seem to have decided on helping him?'

'Because he thinks the Nazis will eventually track Arno down too.'

'That's according to Erich. Have the Nazis been harassing Arno in any way? Erich may be saying that to save his own skin.'

'Either way, we can't take that chance.'

Thomas saw the alarm in Käthe's eyes and responded, 'No we can't. It's time we end this, once and for all.'

28

Later that day, Arno was called in to speak with the lead detective of the Central Homicide Inspection unit. He entered the office to find Karl Nummert sitting behind his enormous oak desk.

'Come in, sit down,' Nummert said.

'How can I help?'

'I thought it was time for us to have a conversation. Tell me, what's the latest on the investigation?'

Arno paused. 'Well, as you probably know, the vehicle we found was registered to Erich Ostwald. The body was destroyed beyond identification pending confirmation by the forensics department, but I have every reason to think that Ostwald was assassinated. I have a name – someone from out of Berlin, most likely hired to do the killing.'

Nummert nodded along as Arno spoke.

'I see. So this is now a murder case.' He seemed curiously distracted and was unable to stop his gaze from drifting to his office window. He was, apparently, less concerned with the investigation than Arno had expected.

'Actually, there was something else I wanted to talk to you about,' Nummert interrupted, as he got up and firmly shut the door. 'Something a bit more delicate. It concerns Bernard Hölz.'

'Hölz?'

'He's has been seen fraternising with senior ranks in the Nazi SA.'

'We've always known Hölz is a supporter of Hitler.'

'Support is fine. Hölz has his democratic right to tick whatever ballot box he prefers. What I'm talking about is something more. He is proving his political allegiance through his work. And that crosses a line.'

'What had he done?'

'The Berlin Homicide Division has an enviable reputation. I don't need to tell you that we live in sensitive times. The future of the department remains uncertain. Two junior officers have reported that Hölz has become increasingly zealous in his work. This is not the time for detectives to bypass the judiciary and hand out their own punishments.'

'Punishments?'

'It seems he likes to use the whip to encourage a confession.'

Arno began to wonder why he had been brought in to be told this. The next thing that Nummert said supplied the answer.

'This is strictly confidential. I want you to keep an eye on him for me. The lie of the land is shifting and I need to know if we have the clear commitment of all of our men.'

'You suspect where his loyalties lie?'

'There's talk of the SA being allowed to undertake police duties. You've probably already noticed that their tails are up. Their commanding officers are looking to make allegiances with agents across the department. Scratching each other's backs, if you take my meaning. Hölz seems to be finding favour at just the right time in his career.'

'Do you know much about him?'

'His details are all on record. The first son of a bank official in Breslau. A high achiever, he completed his Abitur a year early, then went on to study law in Tübingen. He spent some time studying in Berlin too, where he joined the SA in 1930.'

'Hölz was a Brownshirt?'

Nummert nodded. 'Yes. By all accounts he was well-tutored in Tübingen. The university there is very nationalistic and has a low opinion of Jews. Hölz was prominent in the societies, and won several debating competitions.'

No wonder he always paraded as beyond reproach, Arno thought to himself. 'So he's a first-rate supporter of the Nazis?'

'More than a supporter. Hölz's university record is not exactly pretty. He formed his own movement along with some fellow students. As far as I can tell, its only purpose was to spread loathing.' Nummert handed over a sheet of paper. It was a poster, filled with densely printed type.

OPEN YOUR EYES!
You know you have been betrayed!
Consider the facts:
We were undefeated and still fighting on the front
Until a white flag was raised. By who?
By deserters and deceivers!
Who plunged a knife in your back!
How many Jews did you see alongside you fighting in the mud
and trenches?
None.
Yet how many Jews do you see swelling the offices of
government?
The Jewish race has a grip on the levers of power.
Who fought whilst they pushed paper and wrote out cheques to

themselves?
Do you see the deception NOW!
OUR *country should be governed by* OUR *people or risk*
OUR *blood being used up to fight another war just to hand power*
to foreigners.
GERMANY *for GERMANS!*
DOWN *with JEWS!*

Arno read it. His first thoughts were of Monika. With rabid ideas like this in circulation, it was no wonder she and her family chose to leave the country. And knowing now he was sharing an office with someone who'd been a Nazi activist, whose beliefs still bubbled beneath the surface, filled him with contempt.

'Why would the police take him on?'

'We were hesitant to begin with. But he has excellent credentials and the chiefs insisted. Besides this was a number of years ago now.' Nummert took the poster back. 'Maybe a touch of youthful fanaticism here, but with this sort of thing in his track record, I just wonder about his motivations as a detective. Especially if he's being stirred up by the Nazis.'

'I'll dig around,' Arno said.

'I want him monitored, that's all. This is nothing official. I'm not asking you to file any reports. You two share an office, so be attentive to his movements.'

Arno agreed to watch Hölz. Whilst thinking to himself, that nothing would give him greater satisfaction.

Later that day, Arno had a message. The autopsy was complete and he was required to visit the attending pathologist within the next forty-eight hours. An advanced note warned that identification of the victim was near to impossible but that other evidence had been found, evidence which the investigating detective would

174

find useful.

Arno wasted no time in travelling to the grand halls of the police forensics laboratory. His footsteps echoed in the stone corridors that were lined with marble columns. From the reception, he was taken up a wide staircase with a barrel-vaulted ceiling before being led through a glass door and into the laboratory.

He was introduced to the pathologist. Arthur Brockmann was a tall man with a healthy robustness, that suggested that he never allowed himself too much indulgence and never went to bed too late. He had thick blond hair and wore an ambiguous expression that made him hard to read. His winged collar was starched as stiff as ice.

Brockmann took his right hand out of his laboratory coat and shook Arno's with a single, decisive pummel. Arno took a moment to take in the surroundings. Long wooden shelves bracketed to the walls carried dozens, if not hundreds, of different sized glass jars, each of them plugged with a rubber stopper and bearing a white label to describe their contents. A waist-high workbench covered three lengths of the room. On its surface was a trove of scientific equipment, ranging from electron microscopes to medical instruments, interspersed with large pieces of analysis equipment.

Brockmann introduced himself as the lead pathologist of the department, a position he stated with neither pride nor arrogance, but straight to the point. He told Arno that he'd examined the body of the victim, and although the remains were substantially destroyed, was still able to ascertain some core information.

'Despite how ravaged the body was, I was still able to trace some significant indications from what was left of the bones and skull. I estimate the victim to have been between thirty-eight and forty-five years old.

Undoubtedly male, at around six feet tall. In reasonable health, no discernable signs of illness or malnutrition, either during childhood, pubescence or adulthood. The only incidence of physical ailment was found in the lungs, most probably as a result of long exposure to a dusty atmosphere. My guess, therefore, is that he may have been a factory or workshop worker.'

Arno listened closely. All his expectations waited for a confirmation that a description of the dead man would accord with Erich Ostwald. The age range was about right. So was the height. But the condition of the lungs? – Erich was no factory worker.

'So some of the lungs were still intact?'

Brockmann gestured towards a door with frosted glass. 'We have the body laid out next door if you'd like to see it.'

'Yes, of course.'

'Follow me.'

Arno found himself in a side-room stood above an autopsy bench with a white sheet draped over it. A series of lumps and mounds gave the vague suggestion of the crumpled body underneath.

'The most difficult part is in distinguishing between forensically significant trauma and postmortem alteration,' Brockmann continued in his precise manner.

'You mean, whether an injury happened before death or only after, perhaps as a result of the fire?'

'Exactly.'

Brockmann pulled back the sheet. Beneath it was a black-and-grey skeleton that had clearly been sectioned together, since most of the pieces were dislocated from each other.

'You can see, there's barely any tissue remaining, and what's left of the skeletal structure is highly fragmented.'

'And the lung tissue?'

'It's not obvious to see with the naked eye,' Brockmann replied, 'but if you know where to look you'll notice the ribcage partially preserved some of the vital organs.'

'Could the lungs have deteriorated some other way?'

'Being a manual labourer of some sort is most likely.'

'What about smoking – would that account for the lungs?'

'Unlikely. His bronchioles were clogged with fine black particles. Literally dust. I'm talking about two or three decades of exposure to some sort of fine debris that a man might breathe every day of his life.'

'I see,' Arno said feeling perplexed. 'Did you find anything else?'

'We discovered a single shred of clothing upon the victim, the only article that the fire didn't destroy: a section of leather from his waist belt. It was under a buckle but didn't burn. The findings are consistent with the premise that the car and the victim inside had been extensively doused in flammable liquid before the blaze.'

'So you believe an ignitable liquid was poured over the body?'

'At first, the liquid alone would have powered the fire. Then after a few minutes the skin would have split open, exposing body fat, which basically would have become another fuel source. That's how we get to this.' He looked down at the charred remains.

'It's extremely important that we can distinguish between an accident and a deliberate fire,' Arno said strongly.

'Detective, please. I'm not ignorant of the importance of the distinction. We sent a man down to the wreckage, an expert in motor vehicles.'

'Did you?'

Brockmann looked at him quizzically. 'It's perfectly

177

standard.'

'Of course,' Arno said. 'And what did this man find?'

'He studied the remains of the vehicle. Given its state, nothing can be said with absolute certainty.'

'But what did he find?'

'He found that the feeding pipe between the petrol tank and the carburettor looked forcibly loosened. It's possible that excessive heat could have resulted in the loosening of the joint. But his opinion was that it was intentional, for it allowed petrol to flow freely into and beneath the motor.'

'That sounds like foul play then. What about the cause of death?'

'There are several possibilities. We found that the surviving section of the victim's belt had a small fissure in it, a cut or a split, and when we looked at the body again, we found a mark where a sharp instrument has penetrated the hip bone. On closer inspection we found a thin shard of metal embedded in the bone.'

Arno's thoughts went straight back to the knife he had found in the wreckage. It was the link he was hoping for. 'Do you think he was stabbed to death?'

'The blade only punctured his hip by about an inch. It would have been painful but not life threatening.'

'So he was stabbed but that didn't kill him?'

'There's no further sign that a fatal stab wound was inflicted elsewhere on the body. However, the right shoulder shows indications of a heavy blow and the eyebrow bone above it too. The back of the head also has a fracture suggesting further signs of a physical assault.'

'So if the injuries he sustained didn't kill him he would have burned alive. Either way, would you be willing to testify that this was no accident?'

'I would. And that opinion is corroborated by other

findings too. The mallet head found near the car was more than likely the weapon used to club the victim about the head before the inception of the blaze. Being unconscious, he wasn't in a position to escape. He would have been killed by a combination of heat and fumes within sixty seconds.'

'Does the mallet hold any evidence?'

'We found microscopic traces of blood on the face of the mallet, though it's not possible to link these to the victim. But we did identify three human hairs lodged in the woodgrain of the hammer.'

'Hairs?'

'Minuscule strands, hardly more than a pinprick, but under a microscope they are visible.'

'I assume that the hairs can't be matched to the victim either?' Arno was frustrated. It was close but not quite enough. Unless the samples of the victim could be matched, there was too much supposition involved.

'Actually, if I were a court judge,' Brockmann went on, 'I'd want to know where you found your other samples of hair.'

'What of them?'

'Three days ago, I was given a range of objects to examine. A wine bottle. Nail clippings. And several strands of hair. I was told they were part of the same investigation.'

'They were from a hotel room,' Arno confirmed. 'Yes, we gathered them from the room of the suspect.'

'The suspect. Rather, I would say you have the domain of the victim. The hair samples are a precise match.'

'That cannot be right.'

'All I can say is that the two hair samples we examined belong to the same person.'

'The same person? Are you sure about that?'

179

'Forensic science may be a young discipline, Detective...'

Arno began buttoning up his coat, interrupting the scientist, 'When will the forensics report be ready?'

'It will be with you the day after next,' Brockmann said.

'One last thing: if you would grant me a consideration, please don't disclose this to anyone else. I want to be sure I'm the only detective who knows these details – for now at least.'

'Ah. Too late for that I'm afraid.'

'Why? Who's been here?'

'A colleague of yours. Let me see now.' Brockmann checked his notebook. 'Bernard Hölz.'

At that moment, the pathologist stopped talking and looked up. Arno had already left through the swinging door.

29

Arno descended the grand stone staircase with his mind fogged with misgivings. When he returned to his office, he was pleased to find that Hölz was absent. He had the room to himself to consider the full implications of the lab tests.

His solitude didn't last long. A short time later, there was a knock on the door and a clerk entered the room.

'Good afternoon sir. I have some correspondence for Detective Hölz,' the clerk said, a little awkwardly.

'Just put it over there,' Arno replied, pointing to the opposite seat.

The clerk placed a dossier on the desk before disappearing. Arno shut the door firmly and turned the key in the lock. He opened the file and read the typed letter within:

For the attention of Arno Hiller,

Results reference cheque case AH/VH: inconclusive.
On inspection the banker's draft looks genuine. No detection of fraud found.
Caveat: the signatory's account has been frozen for the last 12 months. Checking account is 50,000 marks overdrawn.

Reviewed by the Operations Department, Berlin

Kriminalpolizei, February 1933

Arno was confounded. He leapt up with the file in his hand, unlocked the door and went in pursuit of the clerk. He found him walking through one of the corridors and stopped him.

'Why did you want to deliver this to Detective Hölz?'

'I thought… wasn't it for him?' the clerk said, looking startled.

'It's okay, just tell me, you won't get into trouble.'

The clerk looked around and then hinted in the direction of an open door adjacent to them. They entered an empty meeting room, with Arno closing the door behind them.

'What's going on?'

'Sir, I'm just doing what I've been instructed.'

'And what is that exactly?'

'Detective Hölz was in our department yesterday, milling around,' the clerk went on nervously. 'He wanted to know about the cheque you submitted to us. He became very interested when he saw Von Hessen had signed it.'

'I see.'

'Later, when I was in the archive room, he came up close behind me and insisted that the outcome of the cheque investigation was delivered to him and not you. I objected and said it wasn't procedure and that I could even lose my job. But he said my refusal to do as he said would result in something much worse.'

Arno was seething inside but didn't show it. 'You did the right thing telling me, he won't know about our conversation. You better get back to your post.'

The clerk teetered away. Arno returned to his office in the realisation that Nummert's suspicions were on course. Then, before Arno could sit down, there was another knock on the door. It was Thomas. He came in wearing a curious expression on his face, one that fell somewhere between delight and complete disorientation.

'Busy day?' Thomas asked lightly.

'I've got plenty to tell you,' Arno replied hastily.

'I do too.'

'What is it? Actually, let's find somewhere else to talk.' Arno flicked his eyes to the door as a way of indicating the possibility of eavesdroppers. Thomas got the hint and followed.

They both left the police headquarters and hurried to Arno's apartment. When they arrived Arno noticed something in Thomas' hand. 'What have you got there?'

Thomas held a brown envelope. He opened it and took out a series of photographs. They were the shots he'd taken on the day they visited the car wreck. He took a moment to sift through them before handing the images over.

The pictures showed several shots of the burnt-out vehicle. Arno opened up the walnut cupboard with all the case notes and taped the photographs up. He then put on his wire-rimmed glasses and inspected them. He saw the car, fields, trees and wasteland in the distance, but nothing unusual.

'Look in the background,' Thomas said, 'beyond the car.'

'Which one in particular do you want me to look at?'

Thomas pointed to one in the top row. 'I took that when you were in the woods. Look to the left side. What do you see?'

Arno took the photograph off the wooden door and peered more closely. There was a colonnade of trees and a cluster of bushes. Then, as his eyes adjusted, he picked out a small shape among the shadows. As its form emerged he found he was looking at a figure in the

183

distance. A human silhouette in profile. It looked like a man, moving laterally across the photograph, walking with the line of trees.

Arno rummaged through a drawer before pulling out a magnifying glass. As he hovered the glass over the figure he realised the profile was unmistakable. The slope of the forehead, the pitch of the nose, the way the chin jutted forward and tucked under. Most of all, the wide-brimmed hat.

'That's Hölz.'

'I think he's been following us.'

'Damn him! Hölz is everywhere,' Arno said. 'You have to be wary of him Thomas.'

'Yes, I realise that now,' Thomas answered. 'What news do you have?'

Arno slipped his trouser braces off and sat down. 'I've had the results back from the pathologist. He's examined the body and the mallet head.'

Thomas immediately looked up. 'The mallet?'

'At this moment in time, I'm not exactly sure what to make of it. All I do know is that we may have to reverse every assumption we've made so far. The forensics tests found three hairs lodged into the face of the mallet head. When I say hairs, I mean tiny pinpricks, far smaller than we could ever hope to have seen ourselves. Microscopic traces. But they're very significant. I had every expectation that the evidence would confirm the body to be Erich's. But that's not the case. Firstly, the lungs were riddled with dust. Most likely, whoever it was, he was a factory worker, a welder or a carpenter, someone who was around dust every day of his life. We know that doesn't match the description of Erich Ostwald.'

Thomas shook his head in agreement.

'Secondly, the hairs in the mallet matched the samples we collected from the hotel room.'

'They did?'

'Furthermore,' Arno went on. 'The pathologist identified several sites of injury on the remains of the body. It all insinuates that Mayer was the victim.'

'And the only conclusion we can come to,' Thomas completed the logic, 'is that Erich was his killer?'

Arno frowned at Thomas. He hadn't reacted as Arno expected – neither with alarm or shock. In fact, Thomas seemed barely moved by the revelations.

'Why do you say that?'

'Do you think it's possible that Erich could be as jeopardous as that? To kill a man in cold blood?'

'Where has this idea come from?' Arno asked.

'Just trust me, please.'

'Well, he could have had a motive. He's been in hiding for the past two years. The SA want him dead, or at least there is every reason to think they might. If he could convince us all that he died in that car, then the threat hanging over him would also disappear.'

'So all Erich needed was a body?'

'If he thought his life was in peril, then yes, it's possible that he could have staged his own murder.' Arno paused in thought. All this time they'd been looking for Erich's killer. But the more he considered what the Nazis were capable of and the force with which they were now sweeping across Germany, the more he knew it would be to Erich's advantage to vanish. 'You know, the forensics expert thinks the car's petrol tank was sabotaged. And now the mallet looks like it was used as a weapon. We just need proof that Erich is still alive, which if he is, leaves us with something more difficult to face up to: that Erich Ostwald is now our suspect and our original suspect has turned into our victim.'

'Arno…'

'I need some air. Let's go for a walk.'

A minute later they were walking in the cool rays of the February sunshine. 'If Mayer was the victim, then who do you think it was that we chased away at the Excelsior?' Thomas asked.

'It wouldn't surprise me if it was Hölz. He's getting too involved.'

'What about Erich?'

'If Erich is alive it could have been him, but why would he take the risk of going back to the hotel? You know, I haven't proved it yet, but I believe that Erich's family has a significant investment in the Excelsior.'

Thomas stopped on the street and turned to his brother-in-law. 'Arno, there's something I have to tell you. I know for a fact that Erich is alive. He followed Käthe and spoke to her.'

'What?'

Just then, they heard the sound of footsteps running along the street after them. They both turned to find none other than Bernard Hölz bearing down the pavement. His face was flushed red and he had about him a breathless, excited air.

'Gentlemen,' he announced. 'I'm glad I found you.'

'What is it? Arno asked.

'I made an arrest,' Hölz replied between deep breaths. 'Someone you may know, in fact.'

'Who?'

'Lovis Blume. A friend of yours I believe?'

30

Back at police headquarters, Hölz made himself a steaming cup of coffee and began stoking the coals of the office stove. Arno and Thomas soon followed, with Arno doing his best to reign himself in.

'Why have you arrested Blume?' Arno retorted. 'What has he done?'

'I would've thought you could answer that question perfectly well. He is a common criminal. Try asking what he hasn't done – that list will be shorter.'

'What are the charges?'

'Oh, one thing and another. He was caught stealing a purse from a lady's handbag. Two men from the *Schutzstaffel* apprehended him. When they searched him, he had six other ladies' purses, not to mention a keyring with at least fifty counterfeit keys on it.'

'Is there a law against carrying keys?' Arno said sarcastically.

'Not if they're your own, but you tell me, why would anyone have the need of fifty keys for fifty different locks? Does he live in fifty different houses? Besides which, there was one further thing we found on his possession.'

'What was that?'

'A plan of the Reichstag.'

'That doesn't sound likely.'

'Nonetheless, I'm wondering what exactly a man like Blume would be doing with a hand-drawn plan of parliament, if not for malign purposes?'

Thomas then interrupted. 'You can't arrest someone for having a drawing on them.'

Hölz turned to face Thomas. 'What you fail to realise is that we are entering different times. Radicals lie in wait. Not least the Communists, who would bring down the government tomorrow if they had the chance. The quicker the both of you learn that, the better.'

It was at this point that Arno noticed something about Hölz. The white collar on his shirt had a red mark on it. He took a step closer. The red mark revealed itself as several small blots of blood.

Hölz glanced down at his shirt when he saw Arno looking. He made no attempt to hide the stain. 'Oh that? That will come out with a bit of scrubbing.'

'What have you done with Blume?'

Hölz gave a wave of his hand, as if Blume's fate was immaterial. He was not embarrassed.

'Where the hell is he?'

Hölz invited Arno and Thomas to follow him as he took a staircase down into the bowels of the building. Here, a dozen or so prison cells were used for overnight prisoners. The first two cells were empty. The third cell was dark and had the terrible stench of a cesspit. As Arno peered in, he realised Lovis Blume was slumped in the corner, hunched over like a fallen sack of potatoes.

'Lovis?' Arno said.

Blume, who was turned facing the wall, barely raised his head. Arno gritted his teeth as he held back his fury.

'This man is a potential enemy of the state,' Hölz gloated. 'All means were at my disposal.'

'Speak plainly.'

'Fine. We beat him. It was vitally important that he

188

told us what he knows. Word has come through from the very top – from Herr Hitler himself – that a strike on the Reichstag is imminent.'

'Based on what information?'

'There are reliable sources.'

'From who?'

Hölz stood tall. 'Information given to us by a very capable man by the name of Gustave Jan Ringel.'

Arno began laughing.

'I know him. He's the clairvoyant isn't he?'

Hölz nodded.

'I once heard that these people take their information from magicians, but I never quite believed it.'

Hölz remained more sober in his expression. 'You mustn't laugh at what you don't understand. Ringel has the ability to predict the future. Besides which, his talents are not our only means of gathering information. Sometimes the whip is a more effective method.'

'Let me speak to him,' Arno said.

'That won't be necessary.'

Arno then turned to Blume. 'Did you have a map of the Reichstag?'

All that Blume could manage was a two-word groan. 'He's lying.'

'Yes, of course he would say that,' Hölz said. 'Let me explain to you exactly what we did.'

'There's no need,' Arno said. He knew what Blume would have been put through. Amid the darkness he could see that Blume's ear had been lacerated, whilst the entire surface of his back was a churned-up mass of marbled red flesh.

'We'll get you out of here soon,' he called.

'Not if I have anything to do with it.'

Arno ignored Hölz's remark and squared up to him. 'Make sure he gets medical treatment. What you have done looks barbaric.' Arno led the way back up the stairs. 'I can't go back to the office yet,' he said to Thomas. 'I'm liable to land a punch on him if I do.'

'Let's go,' Thomas replied with a face of trepidation. Together they left the building. Arno lit a cigarette whilst Thomas stood on the cobblestones squirming.

'If I knew what he was capable of...' Thomas winced.

'What's the matter with you?'

'It's Hölz. He rang me one evening and we met for a coffee.'

Arno threw his cigarette down. 'What did you tell him?' he shouted, grabbing Thomas by the collar.

'He said he wanted to help.'

'You told him about Blume, didn't you?' Arno pushed Thomas back and flung his arms outstretched. 'Don't you see? Hölz is trying to undermine me.'

'Look, I misjudged him.'

'Shame you weren't aware of that before. Blume has had the living daylights knocked out of him.'

'I know. And this is what Hölz would also want – conflict between us two.'

'I've no doubt about that.'

Just then, a gust of cool wind blew through the street. Arno turned his back on Thomas and declared he needed time to clear his head. Half an hour later, he found Thomas stood waiting for him outside the police building. When they returned to the office, Hölz was still there, grinning eagerly to himself. 'Your timing couldn't be better. I'd like to know if either of you have heard the name Otto Ostwald before?'

'That's Erich Ostwald's father,' Thomas said.

'You have no grounds to know about him,' Arno said to Hölz.

Hölz smiled. 'I made it my business to.' He was sat

on his side of the desk. From a middle drawer, he took out a file and opened it. 'This is what I know about Erich Ostwald's father.'

'Where did you get it from?'

'I assembled it. Most of it is from the archives office. Otherwise I had to consult old newspaper reports and the like. It just needed a bit of piecing together. I'm rather good at that sort of thing, even if I do say so myself.'

'Bloody hell.'

'Why not? I'm assisting.'

'Is that what you call it?'

'Fine. Very well.' Hölz stood up and carried the file over to the stove. He began to feed the paperwork into the red hot opening.

'Wait,' Arno called. He hated the idea of Hölz knowing more than he did, but then he knew that his rival would be far more adept at raking through the necessary paperwork. Hölz had saved him the task.

Hölz returned to his seat and opened the file. He had the smug demeanour of a school bully. 'Shall I read?'

'Be my guest.'

'I discovered that Otto Ostwald hails from an entrepreneurial family that has been active in German industry since the beginning of the last century. One of his earliest investments was in the transportation of coal between Germany and the Port of Amsterdam on the Rhine. As a younger man, he went into business by himself after apparently falling out with his cousin, whom he accused of embezzlement. Ostwald acquired several of the family-owned coal mines and began trading with outposts in southern Germany and Switzerland. Energy production became his primary interest from this point on. He founded a bank consortium and helped to build one of the first electric generating power stations in Germany. He became a prominent advocate of electrification, and under the banner of the consortium secured exclusive energy supply contracts with districts in Rhineland and Westphalia.

'During the war, he was naturally positioned to become one of the most important suppliers for the army. He was a rich man before the war; by the end of it he was one of the wealthiest individuals in the entire country. And as often happens to men who find themselves in positions of power, he became politically active. He became more prominent in the Reichstag and began to win supporters for his calls for economic imperialism. However, the course of his ambitions changed in 1917 when his firstborn son, Johann, was killed in the war. He then withdrew from political life over the following years and gradually moved his business interests towards entertainment and tourism. He became a major investor in hotels and high-end restaurants across Germany, and one such investment was a stake in the Excelsior Hotel here in Berlin.'

Hölz closed the file and adopted his usual self-satisfied look. It wasn't obvious if his approval related to himself or to the life story of Otto Ostwald.

Arno didn't care about Hölz's demeanour. The fact that he had accurately linked Erich's father with the Excelsior Hotel was enough of an achievement. He took the file from Hölz and looked over the pages.

'The Excelsior makes for an interesting connection,' Hölz went on. 'Don't you think? Otto Ostwald is the sort of countryman you can be proud of. It's a pity his son turned out to be a traitor.'

Arno glared at his colleague. 'Erich Ostwald was no traitor. He informed on corrupt officials of the state. That's the very opposite of treason in my opinion.'

'And yet someone in power still wanted him dead,' Hölz replied. 'Not everyone's idea of a national hero, was he?'

Arno and Thomas avoided swapping glances. They both knew that at a certain point they'd have to reveal what they knew about Erich and the fact that he was still alive.

Still, Arno wanted to gauge how much Hölz knew. He trod with caution as he addressed him: 'I should have more information on the case once I've visited the pathologist. I'm told the report is nearly ready to see.'

Hölz refused to take the bait. 'Please do share your findings with me, when you can. I'd be interested.'

Arno gave a vague nod of the head.

'Listen, about Lovis Blume,' Hölz said. 'You do realise that it was nothing personal? Any other detective in my position would have done the same.'

It was precisely at that moment that a messenger came to the office.

'Sir, news from downstairs. Lovis Blume has just been found dead. Looks like he took his own life.'

'What happened?' Arno asked.

'He hung himself.'

PART V

31

Erich waited outside the rescue home where Käthe volunteered, keeping watch, until at around lunchtime he caught sight of her leaving. He followed her as she crossed the road, then for two more blocks until they were sufficiently lost in the city. At this point, he silently came up beside her and matched his walking pace with hers.

'Don't look at me,' he said.

Käthe's eyes resisted darting in the direction of the figure beside her. She knew Erich's voice instantly. The street ahead was busy with people. 'Shall we go somewhere more discreet?' she said, looking forward with the appearance of talking to herself.

'No, let's keep this brief,' Erich replied. 'Have you spoken to Thomas?'

'Yes.'

'And did he agree to help?'

'He told me that the mallet has already been submitted as evidence. He said there is no possibility of retrieving it.'

Erich was quiet for a minute. They walked on side-by-side, occasionally parting to let another pedestrian walk between them.

'There must be some way of influencing the course

of the investigation,' Erich said.

'If there is then I don't know what it is. Why don't you just leave? Get out of Berlin and disappear? It will be safer for all of us.'

'I can't.'

'Why not?'

'I want my life back. I want to see Ingrid again and I want to see my son.'

Käthe shot a glance sideways. 'You lost the privilege to be a part of their lives when you disappeared five years ago. Ingrid was pregnant when you left.'

'Have you seen her?'

Käthe paused in the street and turned to face a shop window. Erich stopped beside her and pretended to gaze into the same window display.

'Not recently. Thomas keeps in contact with her for the sake of the boy. He feels a responsibility. He is trying to make up for your mistakes.'

'I am grateful. Please tell him that.' Erich looked across at Käthe and caught her eye.

'What are you going to do?' she asked.

'I have an idea, a way for me to return to Berlin. I had it in my mind from the very beginning but as a last resort. Now I see it as my only way out.'

Käthe kept her eyes fixed on the shop window.

'Aren't you going to ask me what the idea is?' Erich asked.

'I'd rather not know the details.'

'There was a story I told Thomas once. It was about a soldier. He went to war but he deserted his army when he saw the horrors of it. He fled his regiment and hid among the lowlands. He stayed out of sight and lived like a wild animal for three years. When he finally decided it was safe to return home, his mother and sister didn't recognise him because they thought he'd died in battle.

They simply saw the shadow of an intruder coming into their house and killed him with a great wooden mallet. It was only when they lit their lamps and looked into his eyes that they recognised him for who he was.'

'That sounds tragic.'

'Yes, but it contains the seed of the idea. A son returns from war after being missing for years. Only this time, he isn't struck by a mallet. He's celebrated for being alive.'

Käthe began to move away from the shop window. She'd noticed two police officers patrolling the street coming towards them. 'You're not suggesting what I think you are?'

'Yes I am.'

'But the war ended fifteen years ago.'

Erich followed. 'My brother never came back. My instinct is that he's dead, but nobody knows what happened to him.'

'That would mean some sort of miracle?'

'It's not impossible.'

'It's too far-fetched.'

Erich dug into his coat pocket and pulled out a photograph showing a soldier dressed in a sergeant's uniform. He passed it to Käthe.

The two brothers were remarkably similar to look at, there was no denying it.

'You have a madness about you, don't you Erich?'

'Look, I want you to get a message to Arno. I need to see him.'

'It's too risky.'

'Arno will come if he believes it is worth the risk.'

Käthe stared into the glass of the shop. It was her own reflection she was concentrating on. She watched herself almost as if she was watching a complete stranger. She knew Arno would be headstrong about helping Erich. Rather than opposing a meeting, the best thing she could do was to back him up.

'I'll see what I can do,' she said.

With that, Erich retreated and immediately stepped onto a passing tram, where he took a seat on one of the long wooden benches. He let his mind skim over his next move. Just like his espionage work for the military police, he was accustomed to the chaos of shifting circumstances.

Later, he wandered through the lamp-lit streets of Wedding district looking for a drink in the most inconspicuous place possible. He made his way through the dirt and bite of the grubbier corners of the city, and down a flight of steps. He entered an old wine cellar that had wooden barrels stacked up in the archways and circular tables over which sultry looking men caked with powder and rouge sat sipping cheap cocktails. The whites of their eyes glinted in the electric spotlights as they looked up to see the new visitor enter.

Erich sat down at a marble table and looked around. He smoked a cigarette and then a second. Before long he was approached by a woman with barley-blonde hair that curled around her temples in cloudy wisps. She introduced herself as Lizzie. She wore an orange dress the colour of fox-fur. Her lips were smothered in crimson lipstick and her fingernails were at least an inch long. 'What will it be tonight, sir?' she said in a voice that was pitched half-way between exoticism and boredom. She placed her arm around his shoulder, at which he turned and stared directly into her eyes. His stony face caused her to release her grip from him. With a sigh, she took a long suck on her cigarette and moved on to the next table.

'Wait,' Erich called after her. 'Get me a whiskey.'

'As you wish sir,' Lizzie said, bowing forward in jest like he was royalty.

Then another voice said, 'You better make that two.'

Erich looked to his left to find a woman sitting down on the stool beside him. As she unbuttoned her coat and pulled off her hat, he recognised her as the redhead, the same woman from the telephone box who several days before had threatened to blackmail him.

'It's you,' he said, as his eyes hooked on to the familiarity of her face.

'Hello Herr Ostwald,' she said with a glimmer of a smile.

The waitress brought over two drinks. Erich snatched one and necked it all in one go, slamming the glass down on the counter. He then rose sharply and clutched the red-headed woman by the elbow, taking her deep into an empty back passageway.

'You don't need to be so rufty-tufty!' she said, throwing off his grip. 'Have you thought any more about my proposal?'

Erich smirked at her.

'Time is running out for you.'

'Who are you?' he asked impatiently.

'Don't you remember me? I work at the Sing-Sing bar.'

Now the recognition of her face came into focus. She was the cigarette girl who'd served him and Mayer that night.

'How did you know I was here?'

'Well, if you want to keep a low profile, what other area of Berlin could be better? It seems you're trying to play dead. I'm only asking for 3,000 marks, which is nothing to you. It will be enough to keep me quiet forever.'

'I don't believe you,' Erich said. 'If I give you a single

pfennig, you'll just come back for more. I know your type.'

'But what choice do you have?' the redhead said, with a broad grin.

Despite her being young and somewhat brazen, Erich could see that she was determined to get something out of him. The Sing-Sing bar attracted a mixed audience, some high-class and some very shady characters, a web of creatures that were more than happy to exploit an opportunity like this.

Erich took a deep breath and looked at her solemnly. 'There's always another choice,' he said, rolling his sleeve up.

The woman then pulled out a knife from a sling in her stocking and pointed it at Erich. He stopped for just a moment and shook his head.

'Don't think I won't use this rich boy.'

Erich backed off, raising his hands in surrender. 'You're not that kind of person. Let's talk.'

The woman's eyes flicked from left to right as her hand began to tremble. She dropped the knife, then turned and ran back into the cellar-house, making her way back through the underground bar. Erich followed her through a curtain of beads and down a wooden corridor, where he stumbled over a small dog coming in from the street.

'Wait,' he called out. 'You're making a mistake.'

She dived into an empty room and hid behind the door. The room had lime-green wallpaper and an enormous brass bed. As she hid, she peeked through the crack in the door and saw Erich stride past towards the end of the corridor where a commotion had broken out. She waited before she crept out and dashed back through the alleyway. Erich saw her leave and went straight after her.

She ran into the street where the upcoming evening was busy with people, cars and horses. When she looked behind, she saw Erich had become submerged into the bustling rabble. Then, just as she turned to flee, she met with the force of a travelling horse and cart which threw her to the ground, knocking her onto the cobbles.

Up ahead, Erich heard yelling and the sound of a braying horse. Then everything paused. 'No,' he thought to himself. He watched from a distance as a crowd of people, including two Brownshirts, gathered around the girl. As she was gently pulled onto her back, a trickle of blood streamed from her head. An ambulance to the nearest hospital was called for immediately and when it arrived the woman was bundled into the back. Erich turned up the collar on his coat and pushed through the flocks of people. To his relief she was conscious.

'I'm her husband and will escort her to the hospital,' he said climbing into the back of the vehicle. 'Hurry please.'

'We're married now are we?' she murmured.

'Just keep still darling. You're lucky you weren't killed instantly.'

'My head hurts. Where are you taking me?'

'Don't worry about that, I'll see you're okay – for both of us,' Erich said.

And with that last comment, the ambulance started up and took them away.

32

The country lane that Arno walked along was lined with leafless trees and the incessant chime of quietness. It was one of those still winter mornings when the sky was an immovable swathe of grey and the sun was but a ghostly imprint in the mist. The track ahead was empty and opened out onto a series of desolate-looking fields. There was a wooden gate, and in the distance the shape of a farmer's plough.

He checked around him, as he had done a dozen times before, to ensure he wasn't being followed. Then he took up a position beside the gate and waited. The meeting was due to take place at eight o'clock. It was fifteen minutes to the hour.

The last time he'd seen Erich Ostwald, the two men were on the same side. This time, if he dared show his face, Erich would be liable for arrest. Now a prime suspect in a murder case, he might face the death penalty if convicted. Arno's primary intention was to lay his eyes on Erich's face and to confirm that he was indeed alive – and then to trust his instincts about what to do next. As yet there was no sign of him. Perhaps he'd thought twice about showing himself.

Arno didn't feel threatened. Not from Erich at least. He speculated whether or not he was being monitored by the department. The risk of being seen was not only

Erich's, but he would deal with those circumstances if and when it came to it.

Eight o'clock arrived and went by. Arno watched a large heron fly over him several times, with huge wings that flapped in slow, effortless beats. When he suspected that Erich was not going to come, he felt oddly reprieved, as if it proved what he knew to be absurd: that Erich wouldn't expose himself to a detective of the Berlin police.

But then he heard a whistle from behind. He turned around and saw a figure approaching. The sunlight rendered the individual a silhouette, and for a moment he thought it was Hölz walking towards him. The figure wore a hat and a long coat in Hölz's style.

Arno put his hands into his pockets and felt the chilled metal of his revolver against his palm. But now, as the sun shifted, Arno could see that it was not Hölz at all. It was Erich. The new arrival removed his hat and the sunlight caught the white flash of a smile.

His appearance was most peculiar. His hair was as black as coal and completely ill-matched to his newly grown moustache, made up of flecks of auburn and grey. He'd lost weight in his face and his eyes sagged with tiredness. Yet beneath those changes, the old Erich was still visible. Whatever complications might ensue from this meeting, he felt instinctively pleased to witness the still-living Erich Ostwald.

Before either one of them spoke, Arno gestured for Erich to follow him. He led the way into a patch of woods so they could talk out of sight.

'You cannot know what it means to be in the company of an old friend like you,' Erich started up eventually, trekking over the wet mulch of the woodland floor.

Arno felt no need for sentimental small-talk. 'Is it

true?'

Erich didn't hesitate. 'Yes it's true, and I won't attempt to convince you otherwise. The man's name was Wolfgang Mayer and I met him by chance in Berlin.'

'And he was staying at the Excelsior Hotel?'

'That's when I knew I'd found the right man.'

'Then you took him to the Sing-Sing bar and brought him into your trust.'

'That's right. He told me his wife had died and he had no children. He was just the sort of individual I was after.'

'How is your conscience after killing a man?'

'I've been over it many times in my head.' There was a long silence. Then he added, 'There is no justification except to say that I felt I had no other choice.'

'I should be putting you in cuffs right now.'

'You haven't tried to arrest me yet, so I assume you're willing to hear me out.'

Arno made no reply.

'Look, I had a wooden mallet…'

'Which has now compromised your plan,' Arno interrupted.

'What is it you know?'

'That the mallet is what told us that Wolfgang Mayer is dead and that you are still alive.'

'People need to believe that I'm dead. I'm going to take up a new identity.'

'Käthe mentioned you ultimately want to return as your brother.'

'Can the mallet be retrieved?'

'No, but we can use the evidence another way,' Arno said.

'How so?'

'There's a detective who works for the agency who's very interested in this case. His name is Bernard Hölz.

He's full of malice and would do just about anything to see me kicked off the force.'

'Why is he relevant?'

'Because if we can encourage him to come to a different conclusion about the case, then we can use it in both our favours.'

Keeping his winter gloves on, Arno reached into his inside jacket pocket and brought out a bundle of scrunched up newspaper. He unfolded it to reveal what was inside. The knife.

'Recognise this?' he asked, glancing up at Erich.

'That's Mayer's knife!'

'I found it in the wreckage. The report from the pathologist said there was at least one knife wound on the body, so Hölz will assume it exists. The thing is, nobody else knows about it except me, and now you.'

'How do we use it?'

'If we can get Hölz to believe he is one step ahead of me. His pride will be his mistake. This will become the knife that murdered Erich Ostwald.'

'You sound confident it will work.'

'It will if it has your blood on it.'

Erich's face took on a different look.

'Give me your hand,' Arno said. He held out his palm to demonstrate how Erich should hold his. 'I visited the forensics lab and acquired some sodium hypochlorite solution. I've cleaned the blade free of any traces of Mayer's blood.'

'Sounds like someone's done their homework.'

'Well, we want this to work, don't we?'

'Wait a minute,' Erich said pausing.

'There's no use being reluctant.'

'I have another idea.' Erich said. 'You must cut into my left cheek.'

'That's a bit rash.'

'Listen. It has to be a clean sweep across my face. Not a graze, it has to be deeper.'

Arno looked at Erich inquisitively.

'Johann was inflicted with a scar across his cheek during his university fencing days. He had a *Schmitte*. He wore it like a badge of honour, a mark of duelling courage if you will. If I'm going to return in his likeness, then I must have the same wound to be convincing.'

'In that case, we must reproduce it. Show me where it should be.'

Erich indicated where the scar began and ended while showing how deep it should be using his pinched fingers. He braced himself, then offered up his face for the act.

'I don't know how sharp this is.'

'Just make it as quick as possible.'

Arno held the knife flat. As he clutched it, he slowly made the incision. Erich clenched his jaw in agony as a two-inch gash began to bleed.

'It's done. Don't touch it,' Arno said, holding the knife whilst he waited for the blood to dry. He handed Erich a handkerchief to wipe his jawline with.

Erich took a deep breath.

'It could have been worse. What if Johann had an amputated leg or something. That would have been a real challenge,' Arno said, trying to lighten the sting.

They both started to chuckle. Arno then wrapped the knife in some new newspaper and placed it in a leather pouch with a drawstring.

'How will you deliver the knife to him?' Erich asked.

'With stealth.'

'You're already risking a lot. Let me take care of it. Give me the knife.'

Arno was reluctant at first. 'What do you have in mind?'

'There's an idea I have that will deal with more than one problem. I'll be in touch. Wait for me to contact you.'

'Okay, but don't leave it too long. And make sure you don't make the wound dirty, we don't want it getting infected,' Arno said, handing over the pouch.

'Why are you doing this?' Erich said as they parted company. 'Why would you put yourself in danger like this?'

Arno gazed back at Erich. 'It's just the way things have turned out.'

'What's the real reason?' Erich prompted.

'You already know. Monika. You helped me free her from the Nazis when they were on the brink of taking her life.'

'How is she?'

'She had to leave Germany. She's started a new life.'

33

Dusk slipped into night. With the bloodied knife now in Erich's possession, Arno found himself drawn back to his old apartment. He took a late night tram that seemed to trundle at half-speed as it slowly carried him across the city.

As he travelled, he remembered his old neighbour from downstairs and her daughter. He'd not thought much of the girl at the time for they'd hardly spoke a word between them. But now, on this cold February night, the suggestion of someone holding him in genuine regard had the call of an invitation.

Near to his old building he came across a newsstand that was still selling papers and magazines. One such magazine had an illustrated picture of an Egyptian mummy on the front cover. The magazine was celebrating the achievements of the English archaeologist Howard Carter and his discovery of the tomb of Tutankhamun a decade before. Arno purchased the magazine and took it with him as a gift.

He went inside and climbed the staircase with its familiar rickety wooden bannister and draughty windows. He went up to the fifth floor, and sure enough, found everything just said he'd left it. He went to the door where his neighbour lived and knocked. It was late but the door opened and the girl greeted him 'Hello.'

She looked different to how he remembered. Her face was fuller and more mature. Her eyes were a deeper blue and her hair was a hazelnut colour.

He apologised for calling so late. Feeling slightly embarrassed by his impromptu call, he handed over the magazine with the Egyptian illustration, telling her he'd seen it and thought she might like it. She took it from him and spent a few moments gazing at the cover. Then she drew the magazine to her chest, said thank you to him, and retreated behind the door.

Arno stood on the landing for several minutes, considering whether he should knock again, but it seemed like the moment had passed. Still, he knocked on the door and waited. Why would she just take his gift and then ignore him?

The door remained shut. Along the corridor he saw the ladder that reached up to his old room; he climbed it and found that the hatch had been left unfastened.

Through the shadows, he could see nothing in the room had changed since he'd last been there. Even the half-collapsed bed with its brown mattress was still in the same place. Then he remembered how he'd once stashed a bottle of beer under one of the floorboards. He'd left it there in case of an emergency. The floorboard was beneath the bed; he pushed the frame to one side and, using his fingernails, prised up the floorboard. Sure enough, the bottle of beer was still there, lying on its side with a layer of dust on it like a dead rat. He took it out and then he used the metal edge of the bedframe to dislodge the cap. It was freezing cold inside the attic so he turned on the stove. Remarkably, it still worked.

He went and stood by the window and drank from the glass bottle whilst gazing over the frosted rooftops and the bellow of a thousand chimney stacks of Berlin. He would write to Monika again, he thought. He would ask her if she ever planned to return to Berlin. It was a peaceful moment. A bottle of beer in his old apartment and Monika swimming through his mind like a piece of music.

Then, all of a sudden, he felt two gloved hands grab him around the neck from behind. Eight fingers pressed fiercely into his windpipe. He dropped the beer bottle, which bounced and rolled on the wooden floorboards. He grasped hold of the attacker's wrists and attempted to wrestle himself loose.

The pain suddenly got worse, clogging up his neck in a burst of suffocating heat. The ambush nearly rendered him motionless; at the same time it forced him to lurch to one side, inadvertently doubling backwards so that both figures gracelessly collapsed to the floor. The grip around his neck momentarily eased. Arno twisted and tucked his body under. At the same moment he felt something warm trickling down his cheek. He'd hit his head in the fall and the side of his face was smeared in blood. His spectacles were lost. The hands on his neck now moved to grasp at his shoulders instead. Arno wriggled on the floor, using his legs and feet to propel his aggressor away.

In the space of a moment he managed to scuffle towards the window and with grappling hands he found the beer bottle and took it in his right hand. He pushed himself up and wiped his shirt sleeve across his mouth. A murky shadow stood before him. Arno didn't hesitate. He smashed the end of the beer bottle and launched at the figure in front of him. The razor edge of the glass sharpened in the city lights.

The intruder took a step backwards. Arno swiped the bottle again. A second step and the aggressor failed to find his footing. His left leg dropped through the attic hatch, followed quickly by the rest of his body, crashing down to the floor below.

Arno picked up his glasses and went to the hatch to look down. His attacker lay in a heap on the floor groaning in pain and clutching his leg. The man had a narrow face and a long pointed chin like a rat. He was nobody he recognised.

'Who the hell are you?' Arno shouted down.

Two ratty eyes squinted up. There was no hint of panic in those eyes, only a cruel and chilled determination. For a moment, Arno thought the man might try to climb up the ladder again and come at him for a second time, so he brandished the smashed beer bottle to ward off the idea. The man glared at him and hissed, 'Jew lover. It's time for you to leave Berlin.' He spat on the ground hatefully. Before Arno could reach him to interrogate his meaning, the rat-man hurried down the stairs, dragging his injured leg with him.

Arno rushed down the ladder and checked between the bannisters to the floors below. The attacker had gone.

Then Arno turned to see the face of the girl stood looking out from behind a half-open door. She was still holding the magazine he'd given her.

'I am sorry,' she said, her eyes wide and frightened.

'You,' Arno said in disbelief. 'You told someone I was here.'

'I had to. They threatened me. You're hurt.'

'Who did? Who threatened you?'

'I don't know. They said they were from the police and that I should contact them if I ever saw you here. They gave me a telephone number to ring.'

'The police? Was there a name?'

The girl thought for a moment, as though she was unsure whether she should say. '*Oak tree*. I had to ask for *Oak tree*.'

'Oak tree?'

'I'm sorry,' she said again, then began handing the magazine back to him.

'You keep it,' Arno said. 'Do you still have the telephone number they gave you?'

The girl smiled and nodded her head as she reached into her skirt pocket and offered a slip of paper. Arno took it. Then the girl closed the door quickly, as she disappeared out of sight.

34

When Arno returned to his office on Alexanderplatz, he could hear voices in heated discussion from behind the closed door. He entered to find Thomas in something of a temper.

'As I recall, the Communists were the ones who gained the majority in the November elections last year.'

'A temporary victory,' Hölz came back. 'Don't forget, it was Adolf Hitler who was sworn in as Chancellor last month.'

'And the sooner we get rid of *him*, the better.'

'We will all get our say. Hitler has called for another election. That puts him in a position of strength, and he operates very well when he's on the front foot.'

'Are you sure?' Thomas asked sarcastically. 'I always had the impression the little Adolf was an agitator, not a leader.'

'Not a leader!' Hölz scoffed. 'I don't know where you get your ideas from. The man is a natural commander.'

'Anybody who wants to abolish democracy is no leader,' Thomas responded. 'Please don't tell me he respects the Reichstag.'

'The Reichstag!' Hölz was really getting worked up now. His eyes were filled with an excited fury. He looked like he was going to punch the wall. 'Who in their right mind respects the Reichstag? You can't run a country by committee.' He glanced at Arno and then composed himself. 'My hope is that the Enabling Act will put a stop to all that.'

Thomas began shaking his head. 'To silence all the opposition!'

'Germany is on the verge of a violent Communist revolution,' Hölz retorted. 'And the only way to stop that is with the Enabling Act. Anybody who cherishes democracy should see that.'

'You want to talk about violence? What about that attack in Potempa?' Thomas thought back to the story from last summer that was all over the newspapers, when a gang of drunken SA men broke into the home of an unemployed Polish worker and beat him to death. His crime? To support the Communist Party. According to the newspapers, his family watched on helplessly as the Brownshirts kicked the life out of him.

'Those men were arrested,' Hölz replied. 'Five of them were put to death for the crime. Don't mistake me for someone who condones random acts of terror.'

'As I recall, Hitler publicly praised those men.'

'Sir, I am a police detective trained at the Charlottenburg Criminal College.' Hölz said pompously. 'I do not like the tone of your accusations.'

'Enough of politics,' Arno said, walking through the room. He'd had enough of being handed electioneering pamphlets and staring up at the huge banners that all the parties had erected.

Arno looked across at Hölz, who was pacing back and forth on his side of the desk. When Arno caught his eye, he stood still.

'What is it?' Hölz asked.

'The strangest thing happened to me last night,' Arno began. 'I was attacked in my old apartment.'

'Attacked?' Hölz said. 'Do you know who it was?'

'I don't know. A common thief most likely. I must have interrupted him.'

'Are you hurt?' Thomas asked.

'Not really.' Arno pulled the edge of his collar down and showed off a blur of bruising on his neck.

'Looks nasty,' Thomas said.

'It's nothing. The other man got off worse.'

'And you really don't know who it was?' Hölz asked again, overdoing his concern.

Arno began to take off his overcoat. 'I've no idea. But he ran away, the coward.'

'I'm sorry about your friend, by the way,' Hölz said, as he opened a drawer in a filing cabinet. 'Herr Blume. The last thing anybody wanted was for a suspect to take his own life.'

Arno's thoughts turned to Lovis. He knew full well Hölz was trying to antagonise him but it was time to keep his anger in check. 'Perhaps it suggests his guilt after all,' he said instead, staying cool. 'It makes me wonder if his entire testimony about the Erich Ostwald case can be relied upon.'

Thomas looked at him with surprise. Arno gave a slight shake of the head to tell him not to say anything. Then, when Hölz wasn't looking, Arno slipped Thomas a piece of paper. It was the note the girl had given him with the telephone number on it. Underneath, Arno had written a line of instruction for Thomas to follow: *Call this telephone number. Ask for Oak tree. After 30 seconds, hang up.*

Thomas read the note. Arno gave a look of consent and Thomas got to his feet.

'Excuse me gentlemen. Nature calls.' He went to the door, turning to Hölz, 'Let's forget about the argument before. We'll call it a friendly duel.' He then opened the door and left.

With Thomas gone, Arno took the chance to speak to Hölz alone. 'I'm pleased to say that the pathologist has confirmed exactly what we thought about the Ostwald murder.'

'Oh? And what is that?' Hölz answered lightly, almost as if to seem impassive.

'The mallet head we found was undoubtedly the murder weapon. More to the point, three human hairs were found on it. We are attempting to match the hairs with various samples we have collected. Soon we shall have all the facts of the case. Did you see the pathologist's report in the end? I know you've taken an interest in the case?'

Hölz thought twice about his answer. 'I heard a brief summary, that's all.'

'I'm glad you know about the contents. It seems that there was an exact match between the hairs we found in the hotel room and the hairs on the face of the mallet. We're working on the assumption that whoever was staying in that room was most likely the victim of the murder.'

'My understanding was that Wolfgang Mayer was resident at the Excelsior.'

'Actually, my gut feeling tells me that Erich Ostwald was staying there too.'

'And why would you think that?'

'Firstly, a man matching Ostwald's description has been seen coming and going from the hotel. We also know he was spotted with another man at the Sing-Sing bar and at least one of them was staying at the Excelsior. The way I am beginning to see it is that Ostwald had been staying at the hotel under a false name for who-knows-how-long. As you correctly surmised, the Ostwald family have connections with the hotel. It meant he could exist in Berlin without being noticed. He could see his son and visit his family. But still, he had enemies across the city and they tracked him down. Mayer was assigned to carry out the murder and was paid handsomely for it, as evidenced in the cheque signed by Hessen. He booked a room at the same hotel, and when the opportunity was ripe he got talking to Ostwald and managed to befriend him. They took a ride in Ostwald's car, there was a scuffle, Mayer used a knife in an attempt to stab Ostwald, but in the end resorted to using a mallet.'

Hölz nodded along, remaining tight-lipped about any knowledge he might have of the knife wound on the body.

Arno went on. 'If only we could lay our hands on that knife, then I believe we would have the evidence connecting Mayer to the murder. Do you think that sounds reasonable? So far we are at a loss.'

Hölz considered the question for a second. 'Are you asking for my advice?'

'Yes, as a colleague.'

'You seem to be doing fine on your own.'

'My next intention is to make a journey to Neuruppin, Mayer's home town. No doubt he has fled far beyond there by now, but there will be people who know him.'

Just then, there was a knock on the glass of the office door. A member of the administration staff came in.

'Excuse me, sir, there's a telephone call for you.'

'For me?' Hölz replied.

'Yes sir.'

'Who is it?'

The staff member gave a faltering smile, unable or unwilling to say.

'Okay, I'll be there right away,' Hölz said. 'Excuse

me,' he said to Arno.

Shortly afterwards, Thomas returned to the office. Arno put his finger to his lips to indicate he should say nothing.

'Hölz had a telephone call,' Arno said as a matter-of-fact.

'Oh,' Thomas replied.

Shortly after, Hölz came back in.

'Was it important?' Arno asked him.

'No, it was nothing to worry about. False alarm.'

'I'm glad to hear it.'

35

At noon the following day, a further telephone call came through for Detective Bernard Hölz. A nameless woman introduced herself as 'A visitor from Neuruppin.'

Upon answering, Hölz listened to the voice on the end of the line in a heightened state of attention. The woman said she had valuable information about a crime and that she had something significant in her possession.

'Is this a hoax?' Hölz questioned.

'Maybe I should be speaking to somebody else?' she said, as the line went silent.

'No, you were right to contact me. What is it you have?'

'A knife.'

Hölz's ears pricked up. 'Can you bring it to me?'

'Yes.'

They arranged a time and a place, later that day. The Excelsior Hotel would be most apt. She would hand over the knife, whereupon Hölz would have the missing piece to the murder of Erich Ostwald, in whose blood the blade was stained. Recent developments in blood analysis meant it would be used to match the blood type to the known details of Ostwald's in the military police records.

At a quarter past four o'clock, a red-headed woman moved through the lobby of the Excelsior, leaving a trail of thick, sweet perfume in her wake. It was the sort of drowsy scent that stayed in the senses and made one's eyes wince. Inside, her nerves glistened like diamonds.

It took some time to find him. He was sitting in a large armchair hidden in a corner of the ground floor. A wide-brimmed hat was hooked over the corner of the chair. The tails of his long camel-hair coat sprawled out like several ginger cats sleeping around him. He sat up when he saw her, adjusted his neck tie and pulled his coat straight around his legs.

She caught his eye. He looked different to the photograph she'd been shown of him. He was thinner, more insect-like.

'Are you Detective Hölz?' she asked.

'I'm delighted to meet you,' he replied, standing up to shake her hand.

She put her handbag beside her feet as she sat down.

Hölz's eyes followed the handbag. 'I believe you have something for me,' he said. He was perched on the edge of the big armchair like a sly predator waiting to take a swipe at its prey.

She pretended to smile. She needed more time to read him. 'You like to get straight to the point don't you?' she said.

'I don't have all day.'

'I need to know I can trust you.'

Hölz laughed to himself. 'That's funny because I was going to ask you to explain why I should believe a single word you say.'

His directness was brazen. The woman looked at him with steel in her eyes. The moment was now. The time to convince him was right here, but first she had to tug back the dangling carrot she'd promised on the phone. 'Well, if you're going to be rude to me, we might as well forget it,' she said, rising from her seat.

Hölz held up his arm. 'I may have been a bit crass. Please sit down. I'll order us a drink,' he said, looking for a waiter.

She resumed her seat as she smoothed down her hair, taking care to keep her left temple hidden where a graze was still healing. Hölz looked her up and down, watching her re-cross her legs, giving him a twinge of pleasure. He could see she was no common woman, quite the opposite. She had the face of a porcelain doll, young and fresh, with large grey eyes. He licked his lips and changed tack. 'Let us start again.'

'I'm taking a great risk being with you today.'

He sat back in his chair and nodded slowly. The young woman saw his expression began to soften, as if he was prepared to hear her out.

She decided to continue speaking frankly. She glanced in all directions and then said, 'I believe I have the knife that was used in the murder of Erich Ostwald.' She looked down to her feet. 'But if I give it to you, I want an assurance that I will receive immunity from any possible charges.'

Hölz nodded again. 'You have it.'

'Very well then.'

'Now please tell me, how exactly did the knife come into your possession?' he asked.

'I am a close acquaintance of Wolfgang Mayer. I've known him for at least ten years. He used to come to a bar that I worked in.'

'Tell me the name of the bar.'

She swallowed. 'The bar? It's in Neuruppin. But you won't find any mention of it in any directory. It's a place where men and women came to meet, if you take my meaning.'

'Did you travel in from Neuruppin today?'

'I took the two o'clock train.'

'I see. And this brothel?'

'Wolfgang visited once a week.'

'You weren't a prostitute there were you?' Hölz suggested teasingly.

'No, I looked after the money. I kept the books and paid the girls their wages.'

'And Mayer? Tell me about him?' he said, as he leaned forward.

It was now that she had to tread most carefully. She could see that Hölz was eager to hear what she had to say and she couldn't be exactly sure of how much of Mayer's personal life he was already privy to. She chose to be brief but could see a change in his demeanour, one that made her flesh crawl.

'He was a quiet man mostly. I knew nothing about his private life except that he had a wife who died several years before. He has no children. One thing I can tell you is that he liked redheads.' She laughed a little. 'He always had a twinkle in his eye when he laid eyes on one of them.'

'That's it?'

'Anything else he kept to himself.'

'But you said you were close?'

'He was a regular. You get to know someone's habits if you see them as often as I saw him, even if their private life remains out of sight. He wouldn't always go with a woman. Sometimes he came just to sit and have a drink, which is when he would converse more.'

'And you got talking to him?'

'Well, he was lonely, as most of the men are.'

'And where does Erich Ostwald fit into all this?'

'I'd never heard the name, not until one night Mayer started talking about a job he'd been offered. He said it was for the Nazi Party and he was very excited about it. He didn't tell me the details, not straight away at least, but I had the sense he wanted to. He couldn't seem to hold himself back.'

'What exactly did he tell you?'

'That he was going to be paid a large sum of money to make someone disappear. Someone from a grand family.'

'Mayer was hired to murder Ostwald?' Hölz confirmed.

'He never mentioned a name, but he said it was vengeance. This man had betrayed the Nazi Party. That's what he told me.'

'Did you know Mayer was a member?'

'No. But then there's a lot about our clients that I don't know.'

'Tell me, why have you come to tell me this? What do you have against Wolfgang Mayer?'

'I know the truth about him. Isn't that enough?'

'But you are informing on someone who you claim to be closely connected to. That is hardly a persuasive position, is it now? What's to say that the evidence you are giving me isn't completely fabricated?'

'He gave me the knife as a way to impress me, a trophy of his deed. I couldn't simply accept a gift like that knowing how he came by it.'

'So he was sweet on you?'

'Mayer confided in me that after he'd stabbed him, he burned the evidence. And then there was the story in the newspapers. So I put two and two together.'

Hölz remained expressionless.

'Perhaps you'd like to see the knife?'

Hölz nodded as he threaded his fingers together.

'Whoever is in charge of the investigation is doing a hopeless job. I heard that a detective from your force came to Neuruppin yesterday asking questions. Little more than a boy I've been told. Yet Mayer is still out there somewhere. That's why I came to you especially. Your reputation, may I say, precedes you.'

'Then perhaps it's time you showed me what's in your handbag.'

The woman bent down and brought her handbag up to her lap. The ends of a silk scarf inside lolled at its mouth, acting as a covering. She swept the scarf aside and then lifted out the leather pouch. Hölz held out his hand to receive the parcel. At first, he used his fingers to feel the outline of the knife through the material of the pouch. Once satisfied, he undid the drawstring and peered inside.

He seemed pleased with the contents. For a moment he became engrossed as he delved his fingers into the pouch and unwrapped the knife. Then his eyes lifted. 'There's blood.'

'The victim's I presume?' she replied.

Hölz returned to the pouch. She watched as he half drew out the blade. He made a deliberate point of examining the tip, focusing on the blunted end to confirm the tip was missing. He passed his thumb over the Nazi crest. Then began smirking to himself, as if to permit his satisfaction. 'Why don't we do this somewhere more private?' he then said. He was smiling, showing off a row of zigzag teeth.

'I believe here is fine,' she replied.

'No. I think you would prefer it if we were alone.'

'Why do you say that?'

'I have a room upstairs. All paid for. I have the key right here in my pocket.'

'You can take the knife away with you. I don't have anything else to give you. I've told you all that I know.'

'Are you sure?'

She didn't like the shift in the conversation. So far the dialogue had been manageable, but now she sensed something was changing. She moved her hands away from both ends of her handbag that she realised she was holding like a shield. 'I'm perfectly sure.'

'The problem,' Hölz began, 'is that you are far less clever than you think you are. Come with me upstairs or else I will have to expose you as the fraud you are, right here and now.'

'I'm no fraud,' she objected hastily. She had no idea what he was thinking and knew it was perfectly possible he could be bluffing.

He leaned forward in his chair and whispered, 'You're very attractive. But on the question of Wolfgang Mayer, I know you are lying.'

'I've given you the knife.'

'Yes, but you haven't given me the truth. I don't want to have to force you to tell me.'

'Really,' she said, pretending to laugh. 'You are confusing me.'

'Wolfgang Mayer is not a friend of yours, is he?'

Her mouth went dry. At that moment she noticed two Brownshirts enter the room, one of which looked directly at both her and Hölz.

'You're the one making a mistake.'

'Did you think your act would convince me? You're feisty, I like that but I can see through you.'

She began to stand up. 'If you will excuse me I need to refresh.'

Hölz leaned forward and pressed his index finger firmly on her knee, keeping her seated.

'I wouldn't if I were you.'

'What do you want?'

'I want you to tell me how you came across this knife.'

The woman waved her fingers at one of the bellboys. The boy came over. 'I have a little headache. Take this coin. I want you to get me an Aspirin. There's a chemist next door.'

She turned to Hölz who was staring at her.

'I have a better idea than that. The room is just upstairs,' Hölz said. 'I think it would be best if we went quietly now. Nobody wants to cause a scene.'

She didn't know what to do. 'If this is your way of seducing me, you must have a very strange idea about women.'

'Maybe you should teach me then.'

Hölz rose to his feet and picked her up by the arm, drawing her close to clamp her to his side.

'Make a fuss, and I'll tell those two Brownshirts that you enjoy the whip. I'm sure they couldn't resist such an invitation,' he whispered to her. 'Come now dear,' he said, smelling her neck. 'Let's see what's to come.'

36

Across the square, Arno and Thomas waited. From their window seat in the café they could make out the entire facade of the Excelsior Hotel.

Thomas was tense. He clutched his coffee cup with fingers that fidgeted incessantly. The more he learned about Hölz and his methods, the more anxious he felt.

'This is a risky idea,' he said after a while of gazing out of the window.

Arno looked at his brother-in-law. 'It is, but it will be worth it.'

'And if Hölz finds out that she's lying? What then?'

'Relax. There is no reason to think he'll find out.'

'I don't know,' Thomas murmured, shaking his head. 'I don't like it. The sooner this is done with the better.'

They both fixed their eyes on the large window pane that framed the view of the Excelsior. They had agreed with the red-headed woman that if anything began to go seriously wrong then she was to do the following: she should call a bellboy over and pretend to ask for an Aspirin, and then send him to the chemist next door. That was the sign they had agreed on. The distress call.

Arno and Thomas kept their eyes fixed on the revolving entrance to the hotel. Any sign of a bellboy and they would enter the hotel immediately.

'How long has she been in there now?' Arno asked.

Thomas looked at his watch and compared it with the large train station-style clock on the café wall. 'Twenty minutes.'

'That should be a good sign.'

'It should?'

'It means they should be talking.'

'I wish I had your confidence.'

'Stop worrying. It's clouding your judgement. We need to be at our most alert.'

Thomas glanced into the room of the café behind them. The place was half-full with a modest midweek crowd. A waiter was wheeling a trolley of cakes around the floor. In the corner, a large wire cage housed four yellow canaries who jumped and chirped persistently.

'Who exactly is this woman?'

'Her name is Clara Fischer. It seems Erich met her by chance. She works at the Sing-Sing bar.'

'So that's how she recognised Erich, because she knew him previously from Sing-Sing?'

'Yes. But the problem for Erich was that she worked out he was still alive when we all thought he was the dead body in the car.'

'She was one step ahead of us all, then.'

'She came across him in the street near the Excelsior and suspected him after news of his death had been published in the papers. Then from what I gather, she started following him around the city and threatening him with blackmail. If he didn't pay up, she was going to expose him.'

'How did Erich persuade her to meet with Hölz?'

'More money. And the promise of a new life in a new city.'

'Let's hope Hölz will believe her story.'

'From his vantage point, he should. Remember, a burnt-out motorcar registered to Erich Ostwald was

230

found in open country. There was no reason for it to be there except from foul play, corroborated by the fact that the car had been tampered with and a petrol canister was found nearby. Let's not forget that the body inside matched Erich's in several key respects: it was the same age, height and build. Only the condition of the lungs was equivocal, but after a raging fire that lasted for hours, surely there is room for doubt over that question.

'The head of a wooden mallet was found nearby with hairs that matched the samples taken from a hotel in which Erich's family has a significant stake and where it is reasonable to assume Erich had been staying. We also found a cheque made out to Mayer, which was signed by a prominent and corrupt Nazi official. As far as our Operations unit was concerned it appeared genuine but we now know the cheque was a fake and planted by Erich.

'And then there is the knife, which as far as Hölz is concerned remains unaccounted for. The body had a knife wound, and the doorman at Sing-Sing reported seeing Mayer with a knife, so there are strong grounds for a connection. Moreover, the tip of a knife was found in the body, and the blade that Clara will hand over is also missing its tip. The same knife has a Nazi crest on the handle. We all know that Mayer was an ardent supporter of Hitler and that Erich was working against the Nazis. I don't think Hölz could resist the opportunity of claiming it. He should take the bait.'

'Especially as he doesn't know that you found the knife in the wreckage,' Thomas agreed.

'The exception of the knife is the key advantage. He may know the same facts as us, but that doesn't mean he'll piece them together in the same way. When he has the knife too, he will make sure he takes over the case.'

'And then what?'

231

'Then the hunt for Mayer continues. He's a killer on the run. Except there will be no sightings, there will be no new evidence. Hölz will be looking for a man who is already dead. His inability to solve the case will torture the smug bastard forever.'

At that moment, through the window pane, they then saw a bellboy from the Excelsior walk out onto the street. He glanced in both directions, then paced towards a nearby shop and went straight into a chemist.

'Shit,' Arno said. 'Come on.'

Arno and Thomas ran across the square to the Excelsior and pushed through the revolving doors into the lobby. They went directly to the café area, where waiters carried silver trays laden with coffee and afternoon cake for hungry patrons. There was no sign of either Clara Fischer or Hölz. The sound of a jazz band playing in one of the restaurants echoed through the space.

'She's not here,' Thomas said.

Arno didn't respond. He went to the reception desk and waved over a member of the staff. 'There is a woman in this hotel who is in great danger,' he said urgently.

'Danger?'

'Damn it – have you seen a man and a woman come by here just two minutes ago? She's a redhead, he's…'

'But sir – there are plenty of couples staying here.'

Arno knew it was helpless. The only thing for it was to search the hotel themselves.

'Thomas, you check the reception rooms. I'll try upstairs,' he said, walking off at a pace.

37

Clara Fischer walked side-by-side with Bernard Hölz, directly past the marble staircase and into the hotel lift. Hölz slid the metal scissor gate closed and pressed a button. The machine jolted into action and it wasn't long before they were three floors up and entering one of the hotel rooms.

A large double bed stretched out into the middle of a carpeted floor. As Clara was ushered into the room, she felt her feet sink into the thick, soft carpet. Hölz was behind her. He took off his camel-hair coat and laid it on the bed. He then placed the knife, bundled up in the leather pouch, into the inside breast pocket.

She was sickened by the idea that he had planned this from the start. The thought crossed her mind that she could attempt to run. There was no chance in the lift, but now she could do it. She would have to get past Hölz and open the door before he pulled her back.

He loosened his tie and began to approach her. She stepped back. He stopped, only to look at her contemptuously. Then his eyes shifted towards the bed and then back on her, making his vile intentions clear.

'Don't even think about it,' she thought to herself.

'Come and sit on the bed. Then you can tell me how you really got hold of that knife.'

'I told you, I first met Wolfgang Mayer in

Neuruppin…'

'Stop!' he shouted. 'The truth, please.'

She glanced towards the window. The flash of neon lights imprinted on the glass as the afternoon light began to dim. Where were Arno and Thomas? They must have seen the signal.

'You do realise that I could have you charged with false reporting? You told me that you came into Berlin on the two o'clock train from Neuruppin today. But I know for a fact that there was no train from Neuruppin at that time.'

'It might have been the one o'clock,' she said. 'I forget.'

'There has been a workers' strike along that line for the last two days. All trains into Lehrter Bahnhof have been cancelled.'

Her heart was beating fast now. She felt the floor beneath her began to hum with the sound of a jazz band from the hotel restaurant. The walls trembled with the sound. Out in the corridor, she heard someone laughing.

Hölz fixed his stare on her. 'I wonder. What makes you think you're so special you can lie to me? Maybe you're one of those self-loathing Germans who would rather connive with thieves and criminals than see our country succeed. Just like that Blume fellow who died in a stinking prison cell with a leather belt tied around his neck.'

She dug her fingers into the palms of her hands as she tried to control her anger. Everyone at the Sing-Sing bar knew what happened to Lovis Blume. 'You have no idea what type of person I am,' she replied as lightly as she could manage.

Clara looked at the man across the room from her, feeling the deepest loathing.

'You're all the same,' Hölz ranted on. 'I know that

234

people have been watching me. No doubt requested to do so by their superiors. They have no comprehension of history or heritage. Only an interest in sweeping aside everything that is traditional and replacing it with a shortsighted selfishness. That is what I see when I look at all of you. Unthinking, self-hating fools.'

'What are you going to do?'

'Oh my little peacock. I hadn't decided until we met. For all I knew, you could have been who you said you were. But it only took me thirty seconds to recognise you as a deceptor. And your little stunt just now proved it.'

She looked at him blankly.

'Oh I have a headache, here go out and get me an Aspirin,' Hölz said, feigning her in a fainting fashion. 'It's an old trick they teach you at training school. I suspect you've been conspiring with Detective Hiller. But it's all over now. He's finished. Arno will be arrested and charged for perverting the course of justice. And you? Your life will be in utter ruins from this moment onwards.'

Hölz proceeded to move towards Clara and in the same motion, he locked the door shut. He did this all so gently and with minimal fuss that he almost gave the impression of kindliness.

What he did next was not so gentle. He grasped her by the wrist and pushed her onto the bed so her legs suspended momentarily in the air. Her winter coat flapped open as she fell and quickly rolled over. She flinched backwards, looking around the room.

Before Hölz had a chance to go any further, she thrust her right foot into his stomach so that the heel of her shoe stabbed his rib cage. He doubled over, but not before grabbing her feet with both hands. She twisted her whole body over and dislodged herself from his grip.

But he snatched her back towards him with the wily

235

tenacity of a stray dog. He towered over her, trying to pin her down as she contorted her legs one way and then another. As he got closer, she spat at him and scratched her long nails into his face in a frenzy. He pulled back, touching his face to find it was bleeding. He grinned to himself as she scampered backwards across the bed. Before she got to her feet, she lifted one of the cast iron lamps from the bedside table. She approached him with the object swinging like a pendulum in front of her. By now he was also on his feet and coming towards her again, adopting a crouched, beetle-like posture of attack.

She swung the lamp towards him but he only caught it in his hands and laughed. She quickly checked around, then ran to the basin and pitcher in the corner of the room. As he launched at her again, she picked up the glass jug and smashed it around his head. He crumpled to protect himself but was distracted enough for her to move past him towards the door. She dashed out into the corridor and along the carpeted floor as fast as she could.

Hölz came after her. She was far enough away from him to easily escape, and would have done so had she not dashed straight past the stairway that led down to the lobby. Instead her sprinting legs took her along the corridor until she reached the far end and a solid wall.

Hölz bore down on her at a more relaxed pace now, padding along the corridor, then slowing down to a confident stroll. His face bore the twisted expression of a maniac.

Clara was trapped. There were doors all around her with brass room numbers hung on the outside. Then she noticed that one of the doors was without a number. She lunged over and tried the handle. The door opened, leading onto a hidden stairway with metal steps spiralling upwards. It was her only choice so she took it. She climbed two floors and emerged through another door out onto the roof of the building.

The roof of the Excelsior was sharply pitched, with small dormer windows that looked like eyes peeking out from under the tiles. The centre of the pitch was cut across by the triangular pediment of the hotel facade.

Clara came through a door that opened onto the tiled roof. The only way was upwards, so she began to climb on her hands and knees towards the top.

Hölz followed eagerly. He was faster than she was and was quickly behind her. She scrambled backwards, her fingers and palms pressing against the grain of the tiles. Traversing sideways, over the curved arch of one of the roof windows, she found the slope of the roof flattened out and allowed her to gain some balance. She became aware now of the height of the building and the city below. The hotel overlooked the great Askanischer Platz that stretched out a hundred feet beneath her.

Hölz was clambering towards her with an unhinged look. His insect-like form meant he could move quickly. She climbed towards the apex of the roof and once there she found herself stood upright. The width of the ridge was just wide enough to steady herself and spanned the entire breadth of the building.

He was soon on the apex and standing with the dusk sky enormous behind him. The city of evening lights spread out below.

'There is nowhere for you to go,' he called out.

He took a step forward. Two more steps and he'd be on top of her.

'I'm glad you could join me up here,' she said. Then, overcome with hatred, she did the one last thing open to her now. She reached into her coat pocket and pulled out a 6.35mm Zehna pistol.

Hölz looked down at the gun. 'You don't have it in

you to use that,' he said confidently, beginning to grin.

'This is for my friend Blume,' she shouted as she pulled the trigger. The recoil of the gunshot sent her hand flying to one side. The bullet flashed past Hölz's shoulder, missing him by inches.

He glanced to his left as if to watch it go by. But the expression on his face had changed now that he knew Clara was willing to use the gun. His legs began to ripple beneath him, as he took a straggling step backwards. Just then, one of the roof tiles slipped and gave away, jutting off the side of the building. Hölz's balance was fatally lost. His body collapsed to one side, as his arms flung out and his head tumbled over. At which he gave out a haunting cry as he keeled over the edge of the roof.

She didn't see the body land, but when the screams from the street began to sound, she knew Hölz had hit the ground.

A commotion outside alerted Arno and Thomas back onto the street. A large crowd had gathered around the body of a man on the pavement. Among the onlookers were half-a-dozen Nazi Stormtroopers, three bellboys from the hotel, a pharmacist from the nearby chemist, and several train travellers and passers-by, all of whom peered onto the inert body with a combination of amazement and fright.

Arno and Thomas pushed through and saw the body of Bernard Hölz unconscious on the ground. They looked up and then at each other, reticent and confused, under the darkening purple sky.

38

'Is he alive?' Thomas asked.

Two local policemen cut their way through to stoop over the body and check for signs of life. A faint pulse and a shallow breath were eventually detected. From within the crowd, a doctor who happened to be passing came to tend to the injured man.

Whispering started up. Somebody said he'd fallen from the roof. Upon hearing this, others looked upwards and pointed, and soon enough were sharing their own opinions about what had just occurred. He must have slipped or was he pushed? Someone said they heard a gunshot. Within minutes, rumours were abound that the fallen man was a maniac on the run. There was no good evidence for this, only the kindling of speculation that quickly caught alight and spread.

Behind the huddle of people, a woman slipped out of the hotel unnoticed. Her hands were cut and her coat was ripped. She did not linger. With the attention of the crowd focused on the man lying on the ground, she moved away without looking back.

She went towards a café on the far side of the square where she expected to locate her companions. What had happened to her on the roof of the hotel was beyond comprehension for now. A small part of her hoped the man who lay on the street floor was still alive, although every atom of her rational mind told her he wasn't.

Before Clara even reached the venue she felt a presence approach from behind. She turned to find Arno coming towards her. He held back and then nodded his head in a single gesture, one that told her that everything was going to be alright. Then from her pocket, she pulled out an object for him to see. It was the leather pouch she'd retrieved from the hotel room just before she left. She lifted the pouch; Arno came forward and she handed it to him.

At this point she remembered the original plan: that she should leave Askanischer Platz unaccompanied and travel directly to Potsdam where she would spend the night in a pre-arranged apartment. Stay out of sight for a week and wait to be contacted. And that is exactly what she did.

Arno watched the red-headed woman disappear into the train station. He would have to wait to hear her full explanation of what had happened; far more important for now was that they should all scatter in different directions. Clara to Potsdam and Thomas to his Berlin home, as if he'd been there all day.

As for Arno himself, he returned to his office on Alexander Platz. Earlier that day, he'd already stopped at a ticket vendor and bought a return bus fare to Neuruppin. He kept the ticket stubs in case someone asked him about his whereabouts for the day. The near-fatal injury of a Kripo detective would undoubtedly bring about an investigation, one in which Arno would surely feature heavily. The question was: would Hölz survive to reveal his side of the story?

Arno decided to stay late at the office. He wanted to be at work when news of Hölz came through. At around nine-thirty, a junior member of staff knocked on his office door.

'There's been an incident.'

Arno raised himself from his chair. He braced himself for the news. But it wasn't what he expected.

'There's a fire at the Reichstag,' the colleague said. 'The whole building is ablaze.'

Arno put on his coat and took himself down the scene. There were fire engines and police cars all across the square, and hundreds of onlookers jostling to get a closer look. The building itself was billowing huge balls of black smoke and the glass dome of its cupola glowed savagely with orange flames from within. The carved motto *Dem Deutschen Volke* ('To the German People') that adorned the pediment seemed to hang on the air like an angel amid the black pall of smoke and soot.

Firefighters hosed the blaze from the street, pointing their water jets into the heart of the building and the chamber where the fire was raging most fiercely. The sound of shattering glass punctuated the air, several octaves higher than the ongoing crackle of burning wood that popped and sparked in the chill of night.

Already there was talk of arrests. Arno chatted to a local policeman who told him a young man had been apprehended near the building. A short time later, the arrested boy was named as Marinus van der Lubbe, an unemployed Dutch construction worker and a zealot of the Communist movement.

'What a day!' Arno thought.

He considered going to the hospital in Mitte district where Hölz had been taken, but the hour was late and Hölz was probably being closely monitored. He reasoned it could be a few days before Hölz was well enough to talk – that was assuming his silence wasn't of the more permanent variety.

Instead, Arno moved with a different intention. He knew that the investigation into Hölz's fall would mean difficult conversations ahead. If Hölz woke up, things could get very difficult indeed.

Arno walked beneath a chilled moonlit sky. In the back of his mind he began to weave a new plan of action. Now, with the fire at the Reichstag, this plan was quickly coming into focus. It was an hour after midnight when he took the last tram of the night, disappearing into the city in the direction of Bernard Hölz's empty apartment.

The following morning, word reached Kripo headquarters that Hindenburg was about to invoke an emergency decree that abrogated civil liberties across the full breadth of Germany. Colleagues predicted that it would mean the legalisation of phone tapping and interception of correspondence. Others wondered about the press, free speech, political assembly, and the autonomy of federated states. It seemed like everything was changing overnight.

'Despite who started the fire at the Reichstag,' Arno thought to himself, 'it will be Hitler who will ensure he benefits fully.'

Karl Nummert addressed a room full of detectives, Arno among them. 'After the events of the past twenty-four hours, the unit is on highest alert. I have every expectation that Hitler's SA will be on the loose this afternoon and into tonight, so there will be violence and counter-attacks. Expect nothing but the worst.' He then paused. 'On another note, I've just discovered that one of our men was seriously injured late yesterday. Bernard Hölz has always been a dedicated servant of the office. It's not certain what happened, but reports suggest he fell from the rooftop of the Excelsior Hotel. At this time I'm unable to comment on whether this was related to the Reichstag fire or not.'

Two days after the fire, Arno sat down with Karl Nummert on a bench in a small park just off Pallasstrasse.

'I wanted to tell you,' Nummert began, 'that we're going to bring the investigation into Hölz's fall to a swift conclusion.'

'How is he?'

'He's still unconscious. If he comes around, he's liable for arrest. We gained a warrant to search his apartment on the basis of recent events and found two-dozen printed maps of the Reichstag in a drawer in his study. Some of the maps marked out the entrances and security levels. We cannot confirm the extent of his involvement in the fire – not right now anyway – but when it comes to the question of Lovis Blume then I think we are safe to assume that Hölz had him set up. I can't allow any sniff of this to get out into the press, not with things being the way they are. The unit needs to be above reproach at the moment. I don't want to speak ill of an injured detective, but Bernard Hölz has to be treated as an aberration, one best left in the past. If he survives, he'll be retired from the force. I want him out of Berlin.'

Arno sat listening as he noticed the trees of the Kleist Park beginning to bud. 'I understand your position,' he replied. 'Hölz's time in the police is over.'

'The Reichstag fire,' Nummert went on, 'has brought a chaos of problems. As you've no doubt seen, the Nazi propaganda machine is operating at full-throttle right now, trying to persuade everyone that the emergency decree is justified. And the SA are rampant. They've arrested hundreds, maybe thousands, a veritable purge of Communists from the city. God knows what torture has been meted out. They've opened a concentration camp in Nohra at an old military school to house their prisoners; we're expected to tow the line and send as many Communists there as we can. With the fire at the Reichstag, it's obvious that the Nazis have a clear route to power. It was just the sort of event they might have prayed for – or even orchestrated themselves.'

Nummert glanced across at Arno.

'That's why Hölz must go.'

'A new era is coming.' Arno responded.

Nummert nodded gravely.

The two men parted. On his way home, Arno knew one thing was for certain: with Hölz out of the way he could file his own report on the Erich Ostwald murder. And instead of Hölz leading the hunt for Wolfgang Mayer, it would Arno himself. Such a hunt would be ceaseless, leaving no stone unturned – yet it would be without results, an endless probing where the case would eventually be filed closed and unsolved.

Presently he passed beside a poster for the forthcoming elections. It read: *You gave those parties 14 years to ruin Germany! Give Hitler four years to rebuild it! You give Germany power and time by voting HITLER!*

Arno was overpowered with a rage of disgust. He reached up, digging his fingers into the paper and tearing it from the brickwork. He threw the shredded paper about him as the breeze scattered it along the street. His only thought was for Monika, knowing that in conditions like this she would never come back to Berlin and, more than likely, he would never leave.

Käthe stood in the doorframe holding a blue leather suitcase. She had packed for a week-long trip, but in her mind she wondered if their excursion might lead to something lasting a great deal longer. Thomas got to his feet and together they left their apartment and descended

to the nearest U-Bahn. They took the train to the end of
the line at Krumme Lanke out in West Berlin. From the
station, it was a short walk to their guest house, and
another walk through the woods to reach Wannsee Lake.
The green thighs of the landscape were stippled with
poplar trees and swathes of unopened blossom sat in the
cherry and apple orchards. All about were crooked rivers
and spring lambs drinking from water troughs.

Where Berlin was rapid and fleeting, the country
landscape was calm and enduring. As they passed along
woodland paths, the lakes spread out into great spaces
cooled by silence. Overhead a band of geese flew,
bellowing their low hoarse chatter. A row of purple
tulips swayed in the breeze.

Over the next few days, the sullen weight of winter
would finally fall away to nothing. The days were
fractionally longer and the sun was getting higher in the
sky. A sense of hope was in the air.

It would not be until late-summer that news reached
them of the miraculous return of Johann Ostwald,
sixteen years after first going missing in the war-churned
fields of Northern France. Where he'd been during the
intervening years was a story yet to be unravelled, only
that he'd been living a simple existence among the
taverns and churches of rural France.

Although his youth has passed, the lost soldier was
ready for the next chapter of his life back in Berlin. He
still bore the fencing wound won during his early life; at
the same time his features seemed to have converged
upon the broader set of resemblances common to the
Ostwald family, similar to his father and cousins. His
return occasioned no grand celebrations, for Johann
himself was said to be in deep mourning for his recently
murdered brother, Erich. A silver lining came in the
form of a new member of the family: Johann had

recently got married, to a striking looking redhead named Clara.

The news was conveyed in a newspaper article in the pages of the Berliner Borsen-Courier:

The eminent Ostwald family of Berlin welcome the astonishing return of their beloved son, Johann, a hero of the war. Sixteen years after his disappearance, recorded as missing-in-action, Johann Ostwald returns triumphant yet bearing the hidden wounds of a private anguish. He will be fêted and memorialised as the prodigal son of a highly-regarded Berlin family. We must all be grateful for his safe return, and in our gratitude remember why he went missing in the first place: the result of a terrible conflict that mustn't be repeated.

Käthe read the newspaper article, lying on her back beneath a September sun on the shores of the gentle lake. She commented that the piece was a fitting tribute. Upon hearing this, the author of the newspaper report, an up and coming journalist by the name of Thomas Strack, turned and passed his wife a thankful kiss.

Thomas got to his feet and wandered down to the edge of the lake. He walked along a short wooden jetty, out and over the water. He came up beside two figures sat on the end of the landing stage. They had between them a small model sailing boat. It was Johann and his nephew. The elder was teaching the younger how to rig the sail and cast the boat out onto the water.

'My brother and I used to play with boats like this when we were young,' Johann said to Thomas. 'When he died, I remember coming down here and standing on this very spot, just staring out over the water. I felt like I wanted to dive into the water and never return to the surface. But I knew it was important to remember him and to live well in his honour. Everything I've done since then has been my endeavour to do so.'

Thomas put his hand on his friend's shoulder, before turning and walking slowly back up the slope. The hours passed until sunset. The young boy was picked by a nurse and taken back to the guesthouse, leaving his uncle alone on the end of the jetty.

Lost in thought, Johann was an outline of black pressed against the dusk coloured lake. His mind wandered through the years, from the golden sheen of the last decade through to the darker trials of the present one. Arriving at this point hadn't been easy. Nor had it been for Arno or all the other people trying to survive in Berlin. The Nazis were on the brink of taking full control, and no one could assume they would remain unscathed. On the contrary, in such vociferous times maybe the real fight hadn't even started. And if the moment came for them to face the greater threats to come, then retribution was sure to take on a different meaning altogether...

FIND OUT MORE

Thank you for reading the final part of the Berlin Tales series.
If you enjoyed this book, you're welcome to leave a review on your vendor of choice.

To find out more about other books and new releases, please visit my website at:

www.chrisjoneswrites.co.uk

Christopher P Jones

Printed in Great Britain
by Amazon